T0279095

RÊVOIR

THE FRENCH LIST

HÉLÈNE CIXOUS

Rêvoir

Translated by Beverley Bie Brahic

LONDON NEW YORK CALCUTTA

PAP
TAGORE

www.bibliofrance.in

The work is published with the support of the
Publication Assistance Programmes of the Institut français

Seagull Books, 2024

Original published in French as *Rêvoir*
© Éditions Gallimard, Paris, 2021
English translation © Beverley Bie Brahic, 2024

ISBN 978 1 80309 387 1

British Library Cataloguing-in-Publication Data
A catalogue record for this book is available from the British Library

Typeset by Seagull Books, Calcutta, India
Printed and bound in USA by Integrated Books International

2. August. Deutschland hat Russland den
Krieg erklärt. —
Nachmittag Schwimmschule.

      —Kafka. *Tagebücher.* 1914

2 August. Germany has declared war
on Russia. —
Swimming pool this afternoon.

      —Kafka. *Journal.* 1914

CONTENTS

I
A FALL

A tale that hangs from The Tale[1]   21 March 2020

When is this going to end? That is the Question she asked herself each time she went to him in the passionate and religious movement that governed her, each year many times since the last time, or the first time, a movement whose aim was to postpone the end, this is her destiny and her necessity: hold on to him—keep him by his hair, by his feet, by his bones above the abyss for as long as she had the strength and the need to do so

What she didn't say: 'Mama, I'm just running out to visit the cemetery,' a word my mother kept at arm's length, not only from her body but from her mind too. 'I stay away from cemeteries,' she would say, 'I am not a candidate,' she would say, 'I'm going to pop out to see the baby.' 'How long is this rigmarole going to last?' my mother says, and 'What are you going to see? There's nothing there, you'd be better off coming with me to the park,'

she too wondered when the park would prevail over the place that her mother said 'rhymes with "nothing-to-see",' 'und

---

1 *Révoir*, unwilling to renounce its circumflex, has kept its French name, formed by compressing two words (*revoir*, to see again, and *rêve*, dream) into one.

die Mutter guckte stumm um den ganzen Tisch herum,' the implication, all the same, was that you couldn't not go, as a young bird flies off one day on its migration, on a day that Nature chooses

The trajectory was a straight line to the unchanging tune of 'from hence your memory death cannot take'—I quote you quoting Shakespeare in your language, I was thinking; 'how would you translate *hence*?' you would say, if we knew where this 'fromhence' is, this 'fromhere' where dead is rendered impotent,

hoping, as she went, that the beloved could not from here or from there be reading her mind, you couldn't not feel you were being spied upon, eavesdropped on by the Shadow of the dead

so, during the entire, totally straight road that led to him and not to it—the tomb—the argument between her and the Shadow flared up once more, 'in two months, they will have forgotten me,' the Shadow was wont to say, 'Not a chance,' she'd retort, 'We'll revisit this,' he would say, she had always taken him at his word, she, humble, would retort, hence your memory death cannot take,

hence is me, *hence* is every inch of this body of mine that bears your imprint, this book whose every page was written, barred, corrected, inspired, weighed, revised by you, your hands, your lips, see this scar? This scar is your teeth—from hence death can win no argument with your teeth, she'd assert, the Shadow was assailed by fear, he asked only to believe her, with his fragile heart he was exactly like King Hamlet's ghost, once a sovereign now a beggar, he concealed neither his fear nor his chagrin, nothing is more naked than these beings deprived of their thickness, he who before death was always too warm now shivered with cold

'I, however, am sure of myself, what accounts for the strength of my assurance, the faint, smiling exaltation I exude, is your need, what strength you give me! It suffices for you to want and I can do it,' she thought

Do you believe, the Shadow says, we will ever make love again . . . the question trailed off

Yet again it returns, the belief question, as scintillating as ever, as mobile, lively, elegant as ever, every scale of it shimmers in the effort to return whence it sprang, for belief is a mental fish, restless, swimming by definition against the current, all the while darting tiny, malicious lightning bolts into the opaque stream

In the great crowd of Thoughts, is any thought more lively, more slippery, less stable and thus ungraspable than this agile species? With belief you may be sure you will never be sure. Belief quivers.

Nonetheless, when the Shadow gave me the Question to watch over, I thought I believed, otherwise would I have been on the road at 7 o'clock in the morning, feeling I had the strength to believe? Your job is to believe, the Shadow would say, mine is to doubt. But doubt doubts doubt and clings to belief, I say. If you want me to believe I'll believe, belief is a trapeze artist, all one needs is to have faith in the higher powers, I don't even need to throw myself into the void, towards belief's trapeze, to believe that we'll make love in ninety years, wish for it and it's as if it was done. Meanwhile, we'll come up with other ways, beyond the reality principle, of making love. There are lots of examples in Ovid's *Metamorphoses*. Once death was behind him like a bad thought, when in the world's eyes Ovid passed for passé, he recovered like a frostbitten flower that springs up again, vivacious and innumerable as ever.

I'm no more afraid to make love with your bones than with your books, I protest.

Last year, when Philia left me, I slept with her, together we wept, at her tears I feared she was sad, who knows where the soul hides during this sleep.

Those cats again! my mother growls. What is it with you and those creatures?

Long live cats! say I. Nothing under the sun is more perfect, as the marvellous Diderot proclaimed, when he described his characters' passion for Nicole.

And who, may I ask, is Nicole? my mother's voice inquires.

The object of Diderot's adoration. If anything is more perfect than this pussycat, it is not man, he said. She is innocent, she is faithful, she loves you and loves you with love, only love.

I prefer to warn those among you who may feel troubled by the lines above that (1) I may, in an attempt to elude my mother's remonstrations, cheat with a quotation, I may throw down a counterfeit or two, but for the rest, I never lie; (2) this tale will need the help and company of father, mother, children, lovers, shadows and cats if it is to progress

all was business as usual on this her twentieth outing with the Shadow, as usual the Shadow telephoned: 'Everything OK?' Yes, I could say. 'What's new?' This time I said, 'A new cat. Not to worry. Our cats have left, but hardly had they disappeared than our-cats came back. Naturally I kept the same names.'

'Time passes,' the Shadow says. 'Time recommences in perpetuity,' I say. 'Some days we think the end has come. It suffices to think the opposite.' 'Continue,' the Shadow says.

The strange thing, I thought, is that, as a body and creature you lie in a narrow bed, it must be said but to one person, while as a Shadow you live and breathe inside me, and strangest of all is this multiplication, the very mystery of human life—however familiar and natural it may be—which propels me to your bed-side—since you yourself can no longer move—in order to make us complete, body and Shadow, dead and alive

If we stop to think about it, this impulse is like a mirror image of cats playing at throwing-collecting the ball they push away in order to run after it in order to push it away again, how we go our separate ways in order to come together again, the way we die only at the cessation of that desire. But driving at top speed with the Shadow at your side down the long road to the grave you are not thinking, you are absorbed in the dialogue whose conclusion you know and are expecting: a passionate embrace

At this point, the Question enters the conversation.

'How and when will this end?' the Question has just landed beside her like an obedient and indecisive dove, it too ageing, it too changing colour and tone from year to year. When? Under what circumstances?

Each time, heart beating, chest heaving, I took the road towards him and the ardent visit that would rekindle us. Such had been the case since the decisive year, 1964, right up to another year, the border-crossing year, 2005, the flame no ashes ever extinguished. And right after crossing that border, without wasting an instant, the voyage with no end in sight began to recommence. You might say it took place perpetually in different ways: she went, to his side, to their bed, to their embrace, perhaps in reality, to their room to their couch in the cemetery, perhaps, meanwhile, in thought, as a project, in preparation. Without interruption. As I write these words, Stop! I command. Stop a moment

But why are you writing in the third person? I asked myself suddenly and I stopped the tale.

Here, I stopped the tale. I was halfway there with the Shadow at my side, and suddenly I had a question, it is the reading police, impossible to evade the interrogation.

I had no choice, the tale says. Maybe it's because of the subject. I was embarrassed

The subject? Is it the Shadow you find cumbersome?

Not the Shadow. The fear of a doubt, of disapproval. Regarding an amorous relationship my mother refuses to believe in. That once dead you still live, she calls this an exaggeration. It can happen that the first person be overcome with shyness, the tale says. The third person is the one who, paradoxically, is least well known and best understood. The freest, the most indifferent to the first person's mistrustful looks.

Sometimes the tale balks, doesn't want to say *I*, it fears or is ashamed, of my nudity or of death.

What reins me in is the voice of common sense, the voice my mother assumes in order to denounce the excesses which, coming from me, annoy her, among which the hairdresser excess and the cemetery excess. These are the two cases where I must cover vital transgressions with a protective lie.

I lie, I say I'm going to the hairdresser, secretly I'm off to see you, I am on my way right to the day when the Question peeps up, I no longer know which day that was. Dispatched on the instructions of Time, of Age, like a sprite ready to demand the Shadow's identity card, proof of domicile, like the spirits of dates delegated to persecutions, of retirement dates, of warrants of life, of entry into silences, of fateful anniversaries

Day broke, the tale was back on the road, I followed it

It was Saturday, 7 March 2020, a morning as luminous and soft as a rosy silk shawl; in one another's arms the cats practised their first billings-and-cooings, sudden almost inaudible pre-modulations, vocal chords as yet unfolded, the two beings share the same miniature vibration comparable to the song of the squirrel, but like an echo that comes before the sound. The echo startles me awake, ravished awake; already the voice! Already dawn, on the road, it's at least the twentieth and perhaps the thirtieth time that I hurry towards you, abandoning the little lovebirds at the very instant they are launching their first words. Again, the knell of the Question: 'This time, unique, unique in its kind, will this time of the voice's coming be the last?'

The last?—What one cannot say to oneself without condemning oneself to death

'Luck is with us,' I thought. Let's talk about the smile: it so happened that the sky was a delicate pink and the shawl I had worn to please him was the vast Indian stole of a pale and delicate pink silk, as if I had cut a swathe of the late summer sky, the road ahead is free, it has the supple contours of a horse's flank, and this time, in year 14 of the new life after the last one rings out along with all the others, gentle, intimate, harmonious, tender, year after year, not a wrinkle or a frown. In less than an hour we are quayside. For once, for the first time, the gate stands open: yesterday was the changing of the guardian. The guardian provides another measure of time: we don't change, we come back, we find one another again, behind us we leave a guardian. Then another. We have been visiting for three guardians. The guardian guards the silence.

We, my love, never change any more. Far away and elsewhere, the times we'd lose each other. We no longer lose each other. That's not entirely true. You, love, don't change. You are faithful to your portrait, the one you gave me the last time, with a quotation from Donne: Here take my picture; though I bid farewell / Thine, in my heart, where my soul dwells, shall dwell. / 'Tis like me now, but I dead, 'twill be more / When we are shadows both, than 'twas before. Here, take my picture. When I am no longer around to defend myself, it will be faithful to me. I leave you my books too, that's all you need, you won't need little me. As if you had said to me, I am not abandoning you, I'm leaving you my shadow. I've never been jealous, but all the same, me, dead, I would prefer that you remain faithful to my ghost. At these words, I balk.

I suspect you of thoughts you were a trifle ashamed of, here's one that flits by, leaving its shy furrow on your face: 'When I catch the mirror attacking me, the sagging muscles of my loosening skin and this treacherous double chin, I don't regret calling a halt before my charm like a tooth falls out.' At this, the wrinkled thought of a diminished flirt, my soul on the fly fires off a frightened thought: 'the fastidiousness with which you regard your wrinkles scares me. Will you still love me when age will have ploughed those furrows on my face that Donne in the force of his rage calls *graves*? When my face is ploughed by the future-not-so-perfect, will we make love?' my anxiety murmurs, and repulsed, head bowed, backs off, thinking: 'At least your ego will have preceded me since the days you began your battle with the chin that makes a mockery of your anxious beauty.

'Your neck having lost its firmness, you can hardly be surprised when mine starts to slump. Look, take my photo, it bears witness to our splendours. And you, shameful thoughts, ashamed

11

of being ashamed, disseminate yourselves in mists on this supple road that carries me back to absolute love.'

And so, in conversation with the cortege of worries that love nourishes from childhood to the final violence, we've drawn up in front of the strange kind of hotel where we meet in secret, as in a dream. The place has the potent simplicity of a Noh theatre. Such is its harmonious emptiness that one may conjure up the decor of any of the episodes that spring from the soul's depths. On this particular morning, the hallucination's potency suggests as backdrop a diminutive castle surrounded by old buildings with, downstage, a desolate quadrangle probably borrowed from the memory of a summer night at St John's College, Oxford. Skirting the building's left side towards your address, one catches sight of the small but irrefutable belfry which makes the castle a church as well; the building is flanked by two giant, skeletal and slightly leaning lanterns in whose presence I recognize what's left of Church and Synagogue, a pair of twins we never failed to venerate in Strasbourg when we celebrated our secret destiny in that city. Within this hallucinated castle-temple-hotel, in the space where researchers meet and work, a lively discussion about Jews, Protestants who are Catholics, ageing Judaified Catholics, has broken out.

Enter Marcel, my forest friend. —Is there somebody there with you? my beloved asks on the phone. —Marcel, I say. —Is he dead too? —He is very much alive, stooped, but still upright. —What does he say? —He says: My willy is dead!

I sense that these words in the forest's mouth ring true and reassure my dead love. —You will never change, I say.

I am careful not to use the forest's words. Me, she, my dream characters, change, let us change, in my dream it doesn't show, in my dream naturally I have my old silhouette, slender, agile, and the same off-white Italian trainers, for twenty years the same pair, nothing changes everything in secret changes

Here, on this very line, the marvellous little Isha character makes her entry into our story. While she crosses the mutism border in order that her voice be heard, delicately I push aside the curtain of your silence. What makes this melodious day different from all the other days?

Today is the day of beginning and ending, a day of arrival and departure a day of levitation and falling

A day of promise and destitution I cannot recount. I leave this to the tale

The Tale: this was the day of the Great Change in H, a change that cannot be avowed, promptly buried alive, gauged on the ground: a matter of a premonitory unsteadiness as she walks along the narrow corridor that skirts the tomb, an earthquake that in a second (perhaps half a one) is a threat to life's innocence, a revolution of volcanic origin and suddenly the soul sees a bloody, unsuspected gap open like the cavern of a woman's sex in the throes of a Caesarean: the door of life and death agape. One sees the lips of the forbidden. That's what she saw.

A second later there is nothing to see. Nothing has been seen. Nothing has happened. Nothing was said. The silence quaked.

Next we made love. As usual. Almost. What happened: my tongue tickling your ear, troubling your big toe, the mystery of each part of the cherished body's awakening, musical, ultra-quick ensemble of little resurrections. What came back like a star, unexpected and marvellous: the underpants. A small, slim, tight-fitting pair of briefs, short, almost bikini, they don't make such underpants any more, the simplest of shells cupping the private parts, we were already thirty years old when it came to me that these were *the* briefs, the ones that stand for love, the ritual, and such was the case. The return of this partner, not an accessory, a secret object, witness, fills me with a deliciously actual emotion, a wave of pleasure, Eros' eternal survival. We are, I tell myself.

And it is a similar emotion, a sensation of the soul's erotic jubilation that I feel when I catch sight of Isha perched on top of the book shelf, risking her life, a catmonkey destined to prowl the heights and edges

The Tale: I forget the worst. The crucial Event. Destiny's hateful intervention. Its sarcasm, its bitter sarcophagus farce. Fate's cannibal teeth. The Veil, there's the rub. The Indian shawl of synagogue-pink silk in which she had draped herself draping the hard bed, on her belly on the stone. Let us follow her. She rises. The wind howled long gusts hungry for vertigo, the wind emits a mocking groan as if sent by gods intent on squashing human flies. The vast shawl, the metres-long swathe of pink sky, whirls, precedes, rolls unrolls like a cloud, grabs her by the foot, twists itself around her. Now comes fear.

During the timeless time of the fall, a sentence makes a hasty entrance and with a banner headline bars the tale:

SHE TAKES A TUMBLE BEFORE THE TOMB

In vain the tale tries to omit it, too late, the sentence has struck. Its bolt and the fall combine to execute a single perilous pirouette

During the time of the fall, one of those abyssal seconds the tale might take pages to describe if one were to demand an account, H seesthinks, broken, what? hand? head? knee? chin, let's take it on the chin, there are falls without a fall, without an abyss, rocks, horizontal, spiritual falls without breakage, falls with staircases, noble falls, silly falls, so tragedy veers to comedy, give me a cliff that bends its terrified head to sound the abyss below, adieu euphoric world, Eros' choreography, crash! bang! how do they talk about that in Shakespeare, poor chipped puppet, wait for someone to pick you up, how many months, doctor, to put this leg back together again, you were curious to know how and when to bring this story to an end? Now—

Finally, flat on the ground with that ugly, vengeful sentence and its cortege of echoes and consequences, a clownish, sad sarabande, she explores the shock left hip right shoulder, head intact, honour not so much. One thought: get yourself up before any importunate arrival without an iota of pity for her ridiculous, humiliating posture, foretelling disaster. Modern version of the death-knell. Gets up? Gets up. Up. Everything still works. Dead? No. Bruises? Mental. Narcissus' castle dismantled. Long fiery wound in the brain. 'Consequences of a fall': long speech, unpropitious, warning, lamentable end, stop, reality check. Takes three steps. And? Everything works. Trembling of the arms and legs. Effect of the shock. Down, at the end of the allée: abyss closed. No one will ever know. Will ever have known. The tale? As the saying goes: put it out of your mind.

What remains: the sentence. Over time, she embellishes her role, she knows what you can do with a line of verse that is as mocking as a theatrical god. She improves the story. The setting's importance increases. Such a fall without a tomb and cemetery, and a background high in epic utterances wouldn't go very far. In time, the value of the sentence increases. In a text it would take on importance. In *Ulysses* it exists already but in a cruder form

I think I could take it as a sign, an answer sent by the central post office of thought to the question of the end. If my mother knew about the sentence, she would add it to the cohort of the subjects of her irritation. And him, the beloved, the dead? I don't know what he would think, all this happened after the curtain fell.

II
SCREAM

I have nothing to report, I say into the phone. It was 20 March 2020. I was not going to speak about my resurrection to the phone. Anybody can fall. The world is on its way out the door.

You are the one who said, 'Everything that opens has something to say,' my editor tells me. That was in *Hyperdream*.

I stick to my preterition. That was all I had to say on that and the following days. If I date this modest statement to Friday, 20 March, it is to put me in my ephemeral place in this empty period that tumbles head over heels like a trapezist who's lost his grip. That at least I could say, I was in a state of total performative contradiction, that I was not managing to be was not something I was going to tell my editor

'Everything that opens, even a suitcase, has something to say,' is what you said, my editor prompted. She thought she was being helpful. I realize I have no suitcase. Depart without a suitcase for the end of the world, can I call that leaving? I left so fast, I broke camp in two hours, two cats, two bags, without a thought, without writing, without a model except for memory's illuminated backdrop of the ancestral exode, generation after generation, my grandmother, my mother, before daybreak off you go without anything, just a backpack, life and death images, you are never prepared, for her death my mother was caught short, it was the wrong day, she expected to die a year earlier at the age of a hundred and two, then, she was ready, later the term took her by surprise, out of the blue, quick I flung her backpack onto her boat, and I no longer have a backpack

To go back to the suitcase:

I am robbed of myself. Nothing to say that might endure as long as writing endures. Nowhere the writing might throw its rug down for the time it takes to weave a sentence. Nowhere . . .

And the salutary humiliation: now, everything loses its sheen, its value, above all its reason to be on the very day of its emission. A thought? Past its sell-by date. The compliments and adverbs of time have taken a beating. Only 'now' works. Because it hints at the conditions of the utterance, my daughter says. All the necessary and natural conditions for the rapid crystallization or maturation of a page or a thought—the momentous made momentary, pulverized.

This doesn't mean I don't write; the writing machine is in instinctive mode, but there is nothing to say, it's as if I were blowing my nose, hardly worth sharing.

The necessary irresponsibility that allows the author to write has been confiscated. Under the weight of a responsibility that sits on her head like a sentence to banishment in one of Shakespeare's plays—such despondency!

I am driven away. *Like the whole world*. Hounded from the world and myself. Like everyone. We've all lost the thing that opens. We're all locked down. Not only all the locked-ins we were accustomed to trampling, not only the eternal locked-in. Everyone and everyone and everyone. Everyone who coughs in one way or another, really, mimetically, anxiously. All afraid. Where are we? All of us, in the corridor. We have never been so alike, we the billions.

Nothing to say, I shut up. Like the whole world. We poor humans can no longer stop saying nothing. The Year of the Slow Inner Silence.

All that remains is to scream. That's the best I can do, I tell my editor

Of a Scream, I can speak. This Scream happened on the night of 19 to 20 March 2020. I want to try to describe this Scream. Never had I heard such a Scream. I was asleep. Or maybe not. I remember I'd entered a small room, characterless, I don't know where, it doesn't matter, what was I doing there, have I time to be surprised, to worry, to wonder? No, because at that moment there was an explosion. The howl left my body like a projectile. I was brutally awakened as if by an attack.

What was that scream? says the shape of my daughter, her nightgown at the door to my room

Quickly, to reassure her, I said 'a nightmare'.

It was very high-pitched, my daughter says.

If this Scream screamed, it is because of the ear-splitting violence of the Scream. It woke me. The Scream frightened me. I screamed, I say.

There was a big Scream and next a sort of little scream, my daughter said

What time of night was that? I ask

Shortly before midnight, my daughter says

My daughter and I danced around the Scream. We were frightened.

It confirmed the state of mental exception I'm in. Like everyone else in the world.

It was a crazy, middle-of-the-night telephone call. Shattering, my daughter says

It woke me, I say, and yet I didn't hear it

It came from you. I didn't understand.

At that time of day, you aren't thinking clearly. We said.

It was a pretty loud scream. High-pitched, it struck me. Not your usual range. There was a decor like in a Poe story. It wasn't a joyful scream, it roused me from my bed. A strident meow. Reports my daughter.

I'd gone into a little room, I say, a nothing room. Had I been able to think I'd have said a small trap. Was there a door? No. A window? No. Vacuum-sealed. Timeless. That's when

Someone

A man   a sort

A Stranger but not all that

It was my third fear. For the first two, I was frightened for and by someone close. I trembled. A Vertigo bumped into me. I was therefore doubly afraid, I was afraid of fear and of the fear of being afraid and consequently, vertigo. This one was different

It is terrible to feel yourself recognize a stranger, I say

You recognize someone you've never seen, but whom you must have 'seen' thousands of years ago, before your era. Before the era.

What was truly terrible was thinking you recognize that this man was composed of several men among whom you thought were one or two whom you'd have preferred never to have known. This man, I saw, was pure *hostility*, the enemy. Quite young, 'in the prime of life,' we might once have said, in the pure violence of man. In manviolence.

What truly spooked me was that this was a *revenant*. But not in the least a Ghost, not the assassinated king. No armour. Rather a suit, classically styled, height 5 ft 9, face normal, impassive, complexion copperish, not pale. This wasn't a walking dead. It was someone who was living. And it was death. A man very much alive. He looked at me. I looked at him. At which point, recognizing him, I let out the Scream.

Into the small hours, I re-examined all of the dream scene's elements one after another, under a microscope, translating.

This man was a resumé of 'Hostilities'. He is polymorphous. In the past he infested me. You never totally rid yourself of such a thing. You repress it. That keeps him in the detritus zone. That keeps him, that keeps him   until he frees himself from the mountain of refuse

It must have been the Virus. I say.

I hadn't dared think about it. So far, I'd instinctively banned the word from my brain

It's not a bad thing to be able to scream, my daughter said.

Do you know what my text is called? I say.

What text?

The one I haven't written.

Virus? my daughter says.

I tell my editor: I can't write. I've been ghosted.

Who ghosted you? my mother says. Those editors again, the ones who stop you living?

Wrong, wrong, I say. Not at all. The Virus ghosted me. Like everyone else in the world. It behaves as if we didn't exist. No one writes any more, I say.

Terrible!—to be locked in a dream after facing death. Terrible. To wake up in a dream with no door no window no wake-up call. It's terrible, 'terrible' is the stone you suck on while you watch Time burn day after day while night after night you follow the Temple's agony, one measly feeble clayey word, pathetic as a garlic clove in the mouth of doctors and midwives during the Plague of 1720 as in 540 as in 1349 as in 1920 as in 2020 one moves like the tortoise trying to escape the flames of the infernal ultimate by climbing very slowly fast with its carapace in its mouth, a naked back and eyes welling tears

the burning salt of silence before the business of the end
after the end after the end's epilogue, how long will this continue
this after after? After this dream begins *the tempest to my soul*,
terror that's what it is: the time of the plague, from one minute
to the next, time implodes dead, like and like

'Terrible?'—is that all you find to say? H tells me

That's all I have on the tip of my tongue, I say, I left so
suddenly I omitted almost everything—I know I know, H says.
I left Paris in such a rush I didn't pack any bags, hadn't I left
unexpectedly, following the orders of numerous despotic Voices,
hustled towards the exit and its equivocal corollaries, its cloisters,
cages, cellars of all sizes and shapes hidden behind the big cur-
tains drawn over daylight's illuminations

a buzz of injunctions, of predictions, advice, harassed by
head-spinning interjections. Go go over here quick what are
you waiting for hurry not there get a move on hurry up!

and my books and my——————I screamed

go go

and my

trousers? one pair is enough go

but my—

don't you hear the last whistle of the last plane train boat
tank

but my cats my cats—I screamed

OK for the cats

25

and food for the cats

OK OK go

and my

notebooks I wanted to say, but the door gaped over the gulf of night and gusts of wind,

I wasn't able to say notebooks

a wind howled: all aboard! all aboard! We're off

I wasn't able to say

I wanted to say without my notebooks and cats I am orphaned from my body and my thought plantations all I am is the cornice of a burgled armoire

I clatter downstairs along with the cats and my mother's Voice perched on my left shoulder, muttering: What's the good of all these creatures that spend their time meowing, you never listen to me

After the fall

Exoduel

The duel was between me and H, my third person. I was divided. And not just between H and me, but also between H and H, a duel to the end. H with my daughter, H without my daughter, H to cats, me with my mother on my shoulder, my mother in her midwife mask and latex gloves, Thought pacing around the apartment saying: Me, the last time. Thought, in the divan corner of the living room who can't stop murmuring: This is the last time you will see—your daughter—your son—your cat—your bed—your books—me—until—————next year, and in the course of this opaque, mute blank of a year how many cherished beings will be obliterated, how many furtive funerals, people die without a death sentence when time draws its shroud across the void,

Does Thought also whisper its threats to my daughter? The French dance atop the volcano, Italy is locked down, who said don't let your cleaning woman in? A friend, my cough is an honest cough, your cough is toxic, I've never read *The Plague* and I don't intend to—My son says I find this very interesting, we are totally in the dark about what to do—Thought says we are deported animals. We once-free humans are like chimpanzees, the first thing we were taught was the handshake, the handshake is a gesture of openness, of welcome, passer-by, keep your hands to yourself, they're poisoned, the hour is nigh, I no longer know which day we are born, the problem is to come out in the world of the other side, must find a way out, I thought, and my mother's voice, always ready to rhyme, like Isha my cat who can't see a ball without pouncing on it, chanted, 'Out rhymes with rout'

which is how, in the midst of the rout, of the no-way-out, I come up with the idea for the Suite without Face and without Date that unrolls the figureless carpet of this desert without trace of a paw or memory: in the scenario where human beings flee, flee each other, don't flee, remain calm, find the exit, and on the other hand weave themselves an exit by means of what's without: therefore this book will be a book peopled by beings who are fearless and honest. I'll find my way with *Dreams and*

27

Animals, my writing masters. Weiterkommen! Weiterkommen! as my mother's simian cousin, Mr Rotpeter, says, not just go not just come, no, go further ever further, undaunted and in the dark

I gave myself the following *Order* for the untested Time ahead:

—Give yourself orders

—Try to follow them

—Have the humility to respect the disorder. Similarly: accept chaos, crosswinds, falls.

—Describe the cat saints every single day. Thusly: Time: 6 a.m. Sky twilit. On my left Isha keeps watch atop the fridge. I watch Isha. With her superhuman powers she shimmers me a glance. What does she see? All I see is the white ceiling and the white walls. She sees the sky beyond the sky? The moon of the moon? She sees, sees further, further. Mystery's incarnation: what is this superpower, grace, beauty, inspiration, thought without second thoughts, all these unexplained evidences? I see: a poem with supernatural powers: of the refrigerator she makes a snow-capped peak.

—Describe the bad days, their charm. That of the Horrible Monday, a whirlwind of contrary advice, categorical, aggressive, a maelstrom biting its tail, dislocation of the spirit, of the breath, racket of the dream called Liberty, upside down, broken, head over heels with the shock, denounced. Vicious clashes in the wings: the decision to depart, the decision to stay, now in favour of departure, now of staying right here: the decision to repent of the decision.

The Awful Monday was still Before. The day was normal. Monday was in its usual place. That was the last Monday, and we didn't know. By evening Monday was as wobbly as a loose tooth. The tooth falls out. Next day, a few chapters ago, is the Very Big Crisis. A brief and violent battle within each of us, whence the din of several altercations none of them in tune. In the distance Tomorrow arrives, masked, swelling under our very eyes. You need to go now. Because it is wearing a mask you don't know it will be the Last Tomorrow. What are you waiting for? it asks. We're not going, I say. Someone seeks the departure, forgets where he put it, rummages through the drawers, the wardrobes, the suitcases, maybe there never was one? Let's go

First Age of the Cage Dream:

And to think we are in Oran! We haven't, so to speak, even peeked outside. I waited for Eric to decide. Why Eric? I say. Because my son isn't accompanying me, the dream says. Out through the window all I saw was the castle's long rampart, a long ribbon of yellow stones, close as the bottom of the dream, this rampart with no beginning or end filled the frame, I was a little surprised, I didn't remember that our district was swollen like a belly with so much castle, all the same kind of stone. I wanted to go and see if there was anything other than this wall, so authoritarian. But Eric who was dangling a little cherry by the stem like the tail of a mouse, was waiting for a drink. It didn't come. In the end he decided to eat the cherrymouse. At which point I uttered: *I am bored.* A boredom as long as a wall of doom. I was bored. Then the noisy chorus of little Algerian girls entered, a couple of them, like a pair of lovers, I thought to myself, hair a bit kinky in fine silver-black threads, sweet innocent hardly speaking save in quick gestures, spirals like a Japanese brush or a school of trout, hard to describe, I followed them, they skipped down a labyrinth of stairs. I lost sight of them. My eyes clouded. Nothing on me, a little summer dress and no pocket lamp. The light was outside. Where am I? I've got nothing, no paper, no help. I had my apparitions. It was a no-exit outside.

The Alarm reminded me that the Plague had dragged this mummified Oran into my home. So, the Rats?

In 2030, in Oran, Paris, the rats qua rats were invisible, but you saw their photographs in all the newspapers

In a schoolroom, the Rat President, a virulent aggressive man in shirtsleeves, puffing on a cigar under the No Smoking sign, demands H's papers, thumbs through them, transgresses, I protest, the Rat says: How do I know who you are? Filthy Rat, a guy Rat. Let's go.

A partial departure

So, we don't go, Insomnia says. So, we go?

On my left those who enjoin departure: P, J, A, especially Ar, H, me, my mother, on my right those who (advise against) forbid departure: H, H, J, R, H, me P, J, my mother

Then we talk, my daughter, H and me, staying 3 metres apart, along with Eve, our life coach. At our side, decades and innumerable generations, a parliament of emergencies and exiles, a butcher shop of indecisive decisions

H says: I wonder what Eve would have said

A says: what would Eve have said, I'm wondering

My daughter says: She would no doubt have said:

And H totally agrees.

And here we stand the three of us on the brink of a dramatic and global turn of events

It was summer and spring, autumn was undecided; in truth, there was neither season nor reason, we walked on

Thought, bringing up the rear, says: this scene happened before, in the '30s in Osnabrück—in '29 already, says Eve, the subject plays for time, go, don't go, go, I'm going, what are you waiting for, don't go, I'm waiting for my sister, not, I'm not waiting

We aren't leaving. So, we leave. The departure happened to me, H and cats like an accident. I was dithering: the dilemma theme: let's go: which way does courage lie, which way fear, cowardice, which side on you on, which side is H on from all eternity, occasionally, this time? Which countries had we the courage to flee, to not flee? Which dark day is it on this Monday without Tuesday without a week, without a day?

Eve: I don't wait for my sister, I left without my mother, I'm not patriotic, I leap aboard the last train, I grab the first flight, I jump on the occasion, I've no destination. Save life.

Am I the descendant of Eve who jumps or the descendant of Omi my granny who refused to budge?

The House, which so far, out of modesty, hasn't uttered a word: am I not the safe house, was I not conceived in order to save lives, am I not the refuge, fidelity, patience, far from wars and ruins, my trees have been waiting for you waiting so long. What do you reproach me? The lack of wars and museums? Internet cuts, storms, what holds you back? Courage

Not the courage to flee, I lacked the courage to say.

At 9 a.m. H says: let's leave, let's half-heartedly pack a few bags. And Eve says: Bags! Good Luck! At 10 a.m. I am hoping for an obstacle, some condition that might keep us from departing without me being responsible. I'm counting on the obstacle to decide for me. The Obstacle says, sorry, I'm not equipped. All signs point towards a departure, a car is waiting, the House thinks only of that, those who might object are asleep, no help in sight. Deadline: 11 a.m. H still has a few minutes to ——— ——, during these minutes, as in the *Nibelungen* or *Tristan and Isolde*, no fateful sign, no false or true sail, decision is inevitable. Eleven o'clock! Thought says. H decides. That means: kills the indecision. H looks at Abraham, the look on his face when he decided to kill the lamb is H's face when she sees herself kill the cat. She says: We aren't going. And the decision shakes itself off like a hen that once again escapes by the skin of its teeth. All that in a lightning flash in the interior scene.

We're not leaving, I say to my daughter. Not leaving? says my daughter. And we shake ourselves off like two hens.

We're not leaving, we say. We need to choose a state of mind in the heart's armoire. What are we going to wear? asks my daughter.

We aren't leaving, I say.

With those words we left

To emphasize Fate's work: it is a beautiful day, the road is strangely empty, the car advances inexorably, the sun sets indifferent, majestic, right on time on the Pont de Pierre, at 8 p.m. here's the House, the land of refugees the cats sleep, the triumph is modest and Thought says: see, no one is left on the 13th floor of Allée Beckett, Paris

Times accursed, times blessed, bless the malediction. You'd love to be able to remember this later. But for the moment, there is no later, indeed, there is no instant.

The second day I tell my son-telephone: the departure caught us short, I didn't think to take the Matzos.

Recipe on the internet, my telephone-son says.

But there is no internet. No Matzos. Matzodo about nothing, mutters my mother.

H and me, having left in haste—not even left, shipped off—I found myself aboard my otherlife, my paper embarkation, and suddenly, my capital life become a sarcophagus, my lifeboat has become my castle. And it was Passover.

III

PASSOVER

Wednesday, 8 April 2020

Bessach

and my mother

The last time Mama / my mother led our departure from Egypt was Thursday, 9 April 2009; as usual, we didn't know it was the last time. Eve was at the wheel; with a hand that trembled as if traversed by tiny electric shocks, she scrawled seven letters, also wobbly, across the white page of the agenda in which she no longer wrote anything except a few bits of words snatched from the jaws of the end, all she could ask her once-firm now indocile hand to trace.

Consult this notepad if you want to know what remains after the storm of the centennial, I tell my daughter. Its base is of blonde wood, that same beech wood in which, when she was a hamadryad, my mother recognized her own body's solid and luminous matter. In 1930 already, having just arrived in Paris from Osnabrück, Eve as a young girl later my mother, without

37

a moment's hesitation ordered from a Polish carpenter, like herself a refugee, an entire suite of blonde beech-wood furniture,

I was born modern, my mother says, hardly had I turned my back on the heavy, imposing and unathletic furniture of the Jonas and Klein families with its sombre, even black-lacquered hue, I invented the future; another refugee from Cologne, I didn't pursue our friendship, taught me to drive,

an armoire with a rail to hang clothes, diverse kinds of drawers, Bauhaus keys, shelves of different sizes,

named the Armoire, feminine in French, it too an extraordinarily practical creature, agile, smiling, a product of the metamorphosis of the hamadryad, endowed with multiple capacities, resembling my mother, in its practical spirit and well-balanced body, average height and surprising depth. The Armoire withstands all historical storms exiles banishments, multiple house moves floods epidemics bombardments indifferences, including a lack of respect, shipwrecks; all in all, it resembles its diversely shaped peers: Noah's ark, stout shoes marked Bally or Mephisto, 1930 Citroën, a boat with four wheels or none.

'one armoire made of beechwood and four rush-seat beechwood chairs,' my mother still has the bill with the carpenter's name, Rawicz, no one can predict the future, there's no address, my mother and Eri her sister rent a little apartment, rue de Dantzig, Dantzig in Paris 1930

How do you say beech in German? That's the Armoire's secret, I tell my daughter, Eve said *hêtre* was feminine in German in French, one should say *H être* or *en être* which becomes *en naître*, these linguistic tricks are part of the Armoire's magic, my mother, embarking on her second century, still took mythological pride in language games,

nowadays the Armoire d'Êtres / the Beechwood Being, has become for my cats in exile a makeshift tree

to get back to the daily calendar on its blonde stand, here are the still-living vestiges of what was a language, still spoken by my mother, and a tale from before any tale, now strewn across a long stretch of dated, otherwise empty squares of paper, mute arid. The problem is a word whose letters I am unable to decipher

Bess–ach, my daughter reads, or *Pest, Fest*—we falter, for the first letter doesn't look like a letter but a petal shaped like a crushed heart. Then the vocable seems to ascend the sheet of paper's smooth façade as if on an invisible ladder and stretch across the entire top of the page for Thursday, 9 April,

then silence till Friday, 27 April whose face has been crossed, top to bottom, by harvest spiders between whose lines we can read the words, *Pesach ends*. Trembling, yet reaching with all their might for the top of the paper. Further along, Monday, 20 April, *14.30 water meter read*, each letter fighting to wrench itself from the memory of what it once was, nothing till 29 May, which says *Shavuot*, a word from a memory Eve shared with Omi, her mother, in another time, another language, not with H her daughter.

I note that for the final stretch of her solo journey, my mother inhabited a very distant childhood like a cradle for end times

Secretly, alone, on the brink of silence, she inhabits an ancient language none of us speak, as if without mentioning it to us and under a different identity, she was living somewhere else now and commending herself to a culture she had never openly embraced

—She wasn't religious, my daughter says

She never spoke those words. Never showed, in front of us, the least sign of belonging to a millenary freemasonry. At the end, having uttered the passwords, she sat down to eat with a ghost people. Thus she taught me that among human beings there exists an impulse of attraction and fusion with one's peers, an irresistible dependency as primitive as a spell, which she called the *Zugehör*. Independence itself, she sensed that at night her person was particularly susceptible to this ancient siren song, by bus or by train dreams would arrive from *Zugehör* and spirit her off to the unknown.

8 April 2020

6 a.m., black

A surge of fear, an alarm that goes off inside the body and emits smoke, inner but invisible. And what, precisely, terrifies is the invisible, the fact that the enemy is *unseen*. You cannot unmask it, it is over there, your back shivers, your blind back, the bull's eye, you are the target about to be struck, it's going to jump on our shoulders rake our arms, our neck.

All of a sudden there It is, it's called Id, or Hid or some such thing, the fleshless boneless arms encircle us, one irresistible, intangible hug and your lungs go flat, your heart meows, you open a drawer, seize the big white pistol that takes your temperature without touching you, with your trembling hand you aim the barrel at your forehead and one second—a quick prayer, a mere two words as in the case of the Shipwrecked in the *Tempest*.

At this point Shakespeare comes to our aid in the form of a scene from the *Tempest* in sixty-seven verses, the most cruel, the most actively overwhelming representation that the arts of evocation have offered us,

to begin with, it's about the end of a world.

How does this event occur? In a single tornado, a few terribly short long, terribly long short instants

Time has a duration beyond any human measure, a super- or post-temporal speed, this is how the world ends, like an inordinate fall in whose course you take an inordinately long short period of time to write three letters, how long the e//n//d// is when you must battle impotence and fatality in order to draw *e* to draw *n* each sign fighting back from the tip of your pen like a minuscule boar, a wild beast but reduced in size, just a few centimetres, with bright green fur that crawls over the wall of the sheet of paper, a little green hure follows the scent

You have no idea how difficult it is to sculpt a letter of the alphabet when you have to move an arm sunk in the leadenness of time, it's as if you had to lift the weight of the ocean to get a mouthful of air

What's going on? my mother's spirit, sitting almost 4 feet away from me, asks. A drowning, I say, or meant to say. And the two words that for all eternity toll the demise of Shakespeare's world, Eve's spirit asks, what are they?

All lost! To prayers! I wanted to say.

Between the two words of hope and despair in the throat of humankind, one can hear the gargling of words drowning, a tempestuous howling from the vortex *we split! we split we split*, adieu.

one could hear

while our life's voyage—for as descendants and pupils of Eve my mother, we have always been en-voyaged we have live-voyaged, we've been on the road—the life the road, Eve always headed straight for life, lifevoyaged all hands on deck, at ninety-five she still strode off to the market with one walking stick, at ninety-seven still vivoyaged following her star chart, and, at that age the ellipsis swerves back to Strasbourg where it began in 1910, and how not to follow in her footsteps, life is over here ladies and gentlemen—

carries on

Until you arrive, reach or return to—who can say—a curve where *suddenly* the voyage, ambushed by nightmare, becomes a *shipwreck* that brings us back in an eyeblink to the depths of the tower of my memory the Sequence-that-Recommences, which is what I call the emblematic scene of all my deaths, the one where tender Clarence falls to his death in that other endless scene in the course of which we die first, before death from an interminable drowning which rolls hours into years with a luxury of cruelty like the interminable, desert shipwreck of the Jewish people, who from one moment to the next are tossed from existence into the formless motionless dateless plantless sands, are there any animal-insects at least? Successive sands, successively the same, devoid of the music of time, of countries of a mirage of a city or a building, devoid of milestones, generation after generation after

how painful it is to drown for a long time, a thousand times sink among the drowned populations, ten thousand men that fishes gnawed, heartsick with envy for the lot of the bones rejoicing in deaths you'd give your life for,

how long is it going to last this dying, the unkind irony of wished-for death, silent siren, follow me darling, no matter how often you try to drop the soul's leash, it doesn't want liberty, die again my love says the dream, die better

in vain you vomit your breath into the water's tall column, the vast air scorns our puny death rattle, you need great strength to earn death, in vain you lose life without gaining death, you must drink a sea of Lethe and then after the last death, the drowning continues, another and another, you'll never wake you'll never sleep again you'll just go on adding death to death on the chain from one death to the next

I've readlived Act I, Scene IV a hundred times, the scene among all the scenes in the House of Shakespeare's vast warehouse of deaths, a hundred times, and without exaggeration I wept a little, a few tears mingled with gentle Clarence's so as to season with a few human drops the sea monster's bitterness, without exaggeration for the first time that I experienced this tormented tableau like a hammer blow to my chest was in May or June 1954,

I was sitting under the wisteria's bloom in my father's garden, some of us, like Montaigne, meet Ovid in springtime, some, like my beloved, meet Montaigne; I met Shakespeare during the slow resurrection of my father, the *Complete Works* resembles the King James Bible, same all-powerful language, same lines putting men eye to eye with their crimes, same betrayals and furious reproaches, same tragic malaise in the civilization brother kills brother kills brother, kills George my father too like Clarence, but I'm not thinking of that,

in this volume that will later accompany the sum of my lives, the order of Shakespeare's works responds to secret laws: thus the first play, in this Oxford 1952 re-edition of 1905, is *The Tempest* Shakespeare's last play, therefore everything will start with a shipwreck, All lost, to prayers, we split!

Lost, prayers, split, *perdus*! Prions! Let's pray! We're sinking

That's how literature begins, with an atrocious, lightning swift sensation of drowning, an interminable descent under the watery floor, and a prayer, literature, brief, bitter gulp of a too-late,

IV

ABOARD THE *ENDURANCE*

*Preparation for the thing
one cannot prepare for*

The morning of 22 March is a summery Sunday with pollen showers, disagreeable beauty and in human land not a soul.

In bird land, perpetual fiesta

Long Walk with Nana known also as the walk to stay healthy. A double walk: foray into the outside world where our first steps falter and set forth; inner walk in which the winged soul, offspring of the post-deluge bird-messenger-scout-postman-envoy, seeks a place to perch, if there is one. Our keplerized brains scrutinize, scrutinize.

All these walks, ignorance en route towards science, occur in the New Time. Will you find an occasion to leaf through them in the time to come?

Already the Pereire Walk, on 19–20 March, one walk among many—we passed a few silent humans—has metamorphosed into the Last Walk of the Old Time. Time Past began at that Walk's end. All that is the past-become-Antiquity the day before yesterday. The day before yesterday was the last, had we known.

Speeded up like a little squirreling animal, I scribble here and there on whatever support I can put my hand on, one really doesn't know where the present is, if there is one, if we have time

NB: it is after the shipwreck, and now and then, randomly, that my various omissions are identified, or not. Our boat is broken, we start over from zero. One example, just now: I *realize* that I *didn't think* to bring my two dream notebooks, the Eve-dreams, the Beloved-dreams. Aboard my ship I find a Bibliothèque nationale notebook with two premonitory sailboats skysea, Triton's children known as 'the last notebook'.

Question: why *didn't think*? Explanations:—

Remarks: notebooks I took everywhere, like my glasses. First Separation of me from myself.

The worst of the shipwreck: shipwreck sans bread sans flour sans water sans fat sans notebook sans everything sans sans everything

Monday, 23 March, 9 a.m., sun with haze, news of the Creation, title: The Promised Light.

The cuckoo is at work, artisan of the call: Present! Present!

Do you know

The First Word I'm going to look up in the dictionary? It is Rail

Rail? you say. I never gave it much thought.

Rail! It's quite a story, it's this beginning all atremble with eighteenth-century excitement, governed by iron bars set end to end, the tracks, the railway

And the ties, the trading of the word back and forth between England and France, *rail* borrowed from French that borrows *rail* from English

When there were still centuries of before and after

Railroads to build

Rails that rail, says my mother, the homonym enthusiast

sans notebook, sans pullover sans identity card, sans chequebook, sans everything, and yet not without help

Not without good ship *Eve*, the House for the end of this strange eventful story, in which we had not yet identified our role

and not without great-uncle Shakespeare with his jokes. Might we then be in the final scene, the last scene of them all, the one that ends this strange, eventful history

Remarks:

Proof that my head is spinning: from Day One of *Eve*'s derailment, I set down my pen on a great upheaval of pads and notebooks, a veritable icepack uplifted lifting crashing down again, for the mind flits like the first dove-astronaut without knowing where exactly to land, here? Over here?

not knowing either what I'm doing, what's going on, from the flustered brain to the disciplined right hand, yoked, that nothing turns from its usual task usual path

overhead everything shudders while at the end of my arm, stubborn, the wrist, the hand, the fingers and the pen, an extra finger, are calm and busy, seeing to the wreck and keeping

As if I were composed of many, including me, H, including Eve

One observation: among humans all the demons are loose, instead of human beings they've become 'mortals' overnight, mortals mortalized mortalizing

Among the birds, however, the usual bliss, same notes played without haste, the simple delights of an agreeably obstinate repetition. An incitement to look up

With whom can I share these clipped-wing, teetering thoughts? I take some Tanganil. Yet another joke for Eve. I can only talk freely to Nana, who is already burdened, in such circumstances the Friend's immortal death makes itself felt, the grinding weight of absence, the verdict of the void. Absent! Avalanches of silence. Tell me something!

What remains: literature.

What is literature? A smidgeon of it was left in the hold of Crusoe's broken boat, in Shackleton's, in Ulysses of Ithaca's, and on and on.

The great specialists are not absent: Kafka above all. What he felt in 1914, in 1915, the complete opposite of what my grandfather Michael Klein felt,

Nevertheless, on 23 March, at 9 a.m. Paris time, life bursts in. A text message from Tima, who lives on in the Before Lockdown–apartment buildings. A neighbour has coughed. The whole tower holds its breath. 'And Madame Azizoulay one floor up is walking around in her high heels.'

At this vision I laugh out loud: 'It was a gloomy, empty day during Lockdown. The sky was blue, for no one. Over the heads of the locked-down residents, Mme Azizoulay was trotting around in her high heels.'

I pictured her: just out of bed Mme Azizoulay applies her lipstick, dons her best dress, her high heels. Or maybe, she steps into the high heels and then the dress. She's prepared. But for what?

'Outside', the Plague rages. As far as the eye can see the streets are empty. Nobody. Mme Azizoulay is ready. Ready for a visit from Mme Azizoulay. Click. Click. Click

For the first time since the ban on laughter, I burst out laughing.

Notable: the telephone has resuscitated. In the House after months of silence the little Arcachon horn, the Olifant trills once more, reconnected by a technician. How sensitive to tears I have always been on the Olifant, Telefant, oh child, oh the last call, the too-late-I-called-you, *le sero te amavi*. I was Roland, in vain in vain I sounded the horn. Years I lived off to one side of life, my ear tuned to your next call, time straining towards life-on-hold-life cut off

The modest individuality of each telephone, the unique signature of each vibration, the familiar sounds forever unforgettable that ring unaltered through the ages and the demises, the horn of my father's Citroën whose sound the dog and I, minuscule on the heights of Algiers the horn heard over mountains and neighbourhoods from the very far off Col Ben Mehidi Larbi for a long time after the star fell to the universe's nether side; the vigorous purr of my mother's old Renault 5, the melodious refrain of Isha in the garden Iwant Iwant Iwant, the voice beyond the voice that sleeps in the little red telephone disconnected after the final aposiopesis, 'we'll find another,' 'other' will have been your last word

And after months without a sound, revived by the online intervention of a technician, it trills again. It is 25 March. I had totally renounced. But who? But who? For years no one has breathed? Since 2005, the little red telephone has been asleep in the bottom drawer of the Armoire. I had given it a tear catcher, a terracotta flask in which a Roman collected his tears. Dring! Dring

Who is there? H runs, seizes the horn that rings insistently. And it is Inès. Inès from Chile, Inès escaped from Chili, locked down in Orleans France, vestige of the Trojan destruction of Osnabrück, an insect, isolated, Inès is bored. A few years ago she was dying, I thought her dead. She has not been dead. Bored, she clings to the olifant that I thought had expired.

Economics of the Big Problem:

To elaborate a conduct, I need to begin my calculations from the hypothesis of the worst. Beginning with the Worst, fashion roads, exits, responses

What is the Worst for H?

There are small worsts and big worsts

The Small Worst: dizzy spells. Cause: the thought of the Worse Worsts. What if you don't have the force you need for the fight?

Essential: stay armed. Keep the Endurance at hand

Worse Worst: illness and hence end. The worst, then, is to die badly, to die before you die, die by being snatched from the people you love, the apples of your eye, cats, think 'buried alive'. It's a much worse worst. Always the fear of a bad death circling

Worst Worst: abandonment of your loved ones, a mutilating separation from the children: cats: dogs.

We already know that the Worst Worst is not to die or death but the long voyage that can make life or death endure for six more months a hundred more months without me, my body without me. What Luck they had, those whose bodies were surrounded, their fear accompanied, some of whom, the newly arrived Shades on Lethe Quay, congratulate themselves on having died just in time

You didn't believe you would die so well my beloved

Radiance

on Wednesday the 25th, late in the day, we search: find find a word to describe the light's intensity, the powder-blue sparkle of the strange sky without pictorial equivalent through the bare branches of the oak tree, a work of art and also a commentary, never have we seen such a sky before, how goes it with the earth?

impertinent commentary sent from Kepler's moon to earthlings condemned to their country's jails, nailed to the sequestered planet.

We've neverseen March glitter like this, a gift from a god! They, the gods, tell us: see our abundance, our luminosity, our splendour, our regular trustworthy economy, our enduring beauty, our innumerable moments of lively, erotic bliss

Like compensation for the ship's foundering, like the firmament after the deluge, something grave and tragic, tragically distinguished like a Noh sky.

'Memory' is our vessel's name. Is it a house? It is a good-sized building, slender, white with touches of saffron, a person, truth to tell, often mistaken for an encampment, for a useful inanimate envelope, whereas it is truly a Living Being of great human value, at once solid, faithful and resistant, a patient almost inalterable animal endowed with an ageless memory. The House is a keep, oh how! a honeycomb for all generations with nearly a hundred and ten years of stores, enough to get us right to the South Pole, all the unforeseens included, cupboards ready for who knows what, and all this studiously, without pretention, without showiness, never expecting congratulations. A chest of chests

Here! Open the pharmacy cabinet. It contains an electrical shop, linens, a whole array of mosquito repellents, pots of jam, diverse creams, rummage, seek! Dip your hands into the Bazaar's offerings, scoop up the utensils. And suddenly, seize some long-neglected object, a box never discarded, a box spared, conceived for an expedition that never took place: an untouched cardboard box with a hundred pairs of latex gloves, as if Eve-midwife-my-mother had once upon a time stocked up for some catastrophe, and also a stethoscope with freckles of rust like the hull of a ship abandoned at its last mooring, I saw that in Iceland; this is, therefore, a landbound caravel, dormant sailing vessel ready to be awakened. Provisions for the incalculable calculated by mymother, Christopher Columbus, the Bedford whalers, Ernest Shackleton, the Prepared, our preparents

Before departing for a voyage with no point of arrival, a hopeful crossing, we embark on the pre-voyage, over nights and months we compile lists of utensils, methodically we take stock, a hundred times we set sail, at the end of the voyage's voyages all that remains is for the trip to begin, not forgetting to remember what we will have left behind. Forgetfulness shadows us, dogs our every step, lies in wait for us, its Big Bad Wolf smile barely dissimulated.

What you have to think about, you must think to think about it, what not to forget, what must above all not be forgotten, Missing Properties whose absences H discovers progressively, the indispensable trinkets, objects without weight whose absence whimpers and meows anxiously:—no ribbons for the cats! Not a scrap of ribbon anywhere in the house.

Cats! Here's some string

no notebooks!   —there are envelopes!

no face cream!

We'll soon be out of jam, says a shy, domestic thought

57

Jam! says an austere thought

Forgotten! Forgotten! Where! Where!

Who cried?! The Notebooks: Us! Us! The Dream Notebooks!

The Dream Notebooks! Forgotten?! How could that happen?!

Sacrificed! This requires an explanation! Leave for parts unknown without my heartstrings! Without the keys to the story, without the point of departure!

So no return?

No promised ribbon for the cats! No Umbilical Cord for the Dreams!

I've already been on this voyage, I tell myself, I'm not going, the voyage is my undoing, severed roots, when was that? A long long time ago perhaps in a dream, before I was born

We think we are the first to embark on this voyage, but so many have already undertaken it and a hundred years ago, I recall as if it was me and my yesterday, it was my grandfather who, dreaming of embarking on *The Endurance*, sends off the Michael Klein application. I am a candidate for the first Antarctic crossing from sea to sea across the Pole, it's the end of March 1914, until July he departs for expedition after expedition, by the end of July all is shipshape when suddenly you recall War looming up, dark clouds on the horizon, suddenly you no longer see Weddell Sea Ross Sea, a telegram: we are unable to consider a German candidate, on 8 August *The Endurance* sets sail, on 9 August Michael Klein enrols in the German army, I am aware that our departure has given rise to criticism the 9th I read in the paper: full mobilization,

The word *Mobilization* suddenly assails the human heart, I was two years old when it planted its lightning nib in mine, overnight a soldier steps into my father's boots, off we head for latitude zero longitude zero below zero, zero dead ahead, over there where there was a city or country: the gauzy white-out of an absence of country

On the first days of March, a storm blows our story off course. On the 26th, the weather is cold and clear, we think we see a succession of parhelia. Energetic: Cuckoo! Cuckoo. No explanation: my difficulty in arranging time in its daily slices, as if time was a single loaf, means the dough of one day runs into the next no landmarks, yet each day is different. This impression is owing to the sensation of moving in place, within the turbulence, as if we were on a ship mid-ocean, the terrestrial world being totally confiscated during a crossing with no clear end in sight

In the desert, the Jews felt the same mummification of time, an ongoing incarceration in a featureless landscape with a yellowish backdrop. Forward march if you can, for one is meant to go in some direction, over and over the same kilometre restarts, the crosscurrent is strong as a prison wall.

No trip without dogs. On the *Endurance* the enthusiastic dogs, the ardent men, ardently, enthusiastically study the dogs. All winter all spring. We drift. No one is forgotten. Least of all the dogs. All summer. Sometimes we drift backwards, sometimes we progress is our impression. The wind turns. To the West. To the East. All excited, the dogs look. For a passage. A little iceberg. The same little iceberg. Opening. Dunes. The same ones.

The mobilization. In 1939 the word pierces me like a star. It has never since abandoned my verbal territory. The mobilization immobilizes millions of individuals overnight. Brutal icing up of a population that was partying just the previous night

The cats seek. Find.

H calls: Nana! I've received something! Something got through. Arrived. That a thing turns up in these motionless times is as promising as the fluttering flight of a dove, where are we headed? Where?

Nana: Oh! Who sent *It*?

Whatever else *It* may be, it is the messiah

A notebook! And not just any notebook! *The* Notebook. A noble subject, harmoniously sized, skin ivory, brow adorned with Shakespeare's bust, gilded edges. Greedily I count the pages. They are like thick slices of bread. A wad of banknotes. All the gold in the world, enchanted gold, the bottomless chest, the alchemical crucible. Robinson finds it when, having searched the wreck from top to bottom, he has lost hope. I mistook the holy Thing for a printed book. Nine days ago, I notice it is not on the shelf in its veil of gold between a Diderot volume and a

Shakespeare glossary. A Bible even, matrix of everybook, in invisible ink. Here is the place I lacked.

The House is a surprise post office. The parcel received with joy. H and I now have what we need to survive. I open it. I stroke it. You can touch. In this world without touch, here is something to hold onto. All the blue tits raise their voices in song. Feverishly four flying ants come and go on the sugary page

The cats practice their trapeze act on my mother's armoire. Its facade offers nothing to grip. From the ground they calculate the height to be covered in one leap. just a little over 8 feet. Motor! Up they go! Down again at top speed like skaters, themselves (the cats) their own blades. Computed to a tenth of a millimetre. Write like that, find the right word to a hundredth of a millimetre, leap with a speed that seems as effortless as a kind of slow motion

On Saturday, 28 March, I dream the dream entitled The Most Beautiful Day in the World.

Omi my German grandmother alias my mother of old who wants to 'go on a lovely outing,' in her 95th year. We think of a restaurant that has just reopened, a little article in *Le Monde* mentions it. Very chic, an antiquity, a hundred or so years old. My grandmother looks elegant. I warn her: we'll have to walk— in time. I show her the way on a magic video. We can do it. It will be an adventure. The way is long and steep. She's not fazed. Gaily she tells me, I took a walk like that forty years ago, in the twentieth century, so let's go. We prepare the car. Perhaps she was driving. Omi later-my-mother was always at the wheel. They called it the wheel. In reality, the long road was short as life. Omi—therefore Eve got down. The problem of the car and how to park it vanished, the dream of a valet was on hand for such details. Similarly, the dream had reserved us a table. A suite of rooms full of people, in the last room, which was also the first, the maître d'hôtel greeted us. We were handed two menus. I recognized the voyage of the Odyssey. We peruse it and keep walking. The menu stands for destiny's various courses. I explain the rules to Omi. What was good, what to avoid. She was preoccupied and a little out of her depth. I didn't mention Charybdis or Scylla. This was going to be expensive. Too bad, I thought. For once. And Omi will pay. We leave. Nor did I mention the Nazis. All in all, I was frightened of the monsters especially as chance seemed to be steering us in their direction. People strolled about waiting for their turn. Eating is all travellers think of, I thought. On we go. Mountains loomed up, foothills to peaks. I remember that time we were together twenty years ago, your head on my knees, me stroking your curls, Omi didn't know who you were, it was all so sweet like the sweetest of dreams. Suddenly, on the canvas' right side a cloud event was depicted in sweeping rust-coloured brushstrokes. People raised their heads to observe the phenomenon. Hand in hand we walked in their direction. All of this was very beautiful. I felt so joyous. Elated, I saw that today was a golden day, one that I would later recall with emotion.

I dreamt the dream I believe I'll remember for a long time like a golden dream. I was with the dead and the gods. The dead at my side and the gods behind the curtain that had been hastily painted. But the night before everything was grey, perturbed, threatening, already dead and out of reach of any future. The world was busy with its burial and no one to say I was here, the day will come, I will remember, the air was heavy with ambiguous, last-will-and-testament words. Papers were being drawn up for perjury-free signatures. SMSes did the rounds promising a future in the present you are / will have been / my daughter / my fiancé / my sovereign good / the only one (masculine) / the only one (feminine) / will find / again / for life, with the insertion in each affirmation of the adverb *truly*, one felt that the need to consolidate the degree of truth had increased in the heart of most of the passengers of the ship World, the last words were on everyone's mind,

Readings of the dream:

Gratitude for the Dream that brings Omi back to us and us back to Omi, to the brief and gentle golden age of Arcachon on Tuesday, 17 March, 1960 pre-real fiction

We arrive on Tuesday, 17 March 2020

Later

we will remember / forever

From the heights of Gambetta-Hugo I showed Omi, an ancient divinity exiled from Germany, the sea over there on earth as in heaven. In the marketplace, the fish glow like embers, and all around us years of happiness lithe and tall as pine trees, I seduced her, I played the siren, Arcachon on the Rhine, I pointed out where at the end of the avenue gauzy clouds festooned the web of time to come, I said: 'chocolate, sunset, ice cream, bridge, Krimi' I lured her: 'Arcachon is like Osnabrück minus the Nazis', so she came and we built a house to fit, she was a tiny woman

May we one day reach the promised later. Were we to get there, we'd never forget.

I shall write: 'they remembered the day when they remembered one childhood after another, it was just before the disappearance of the old memory,' I told myself. I'd like to be able truly to write—remember.

In fact, I never remember anything about what really happened: my memory only keeps alive what is written in books.

The cats, goddesses of the Present enjoy, enjoy, desire congratulations receive congratulations

Here: the poignant charm of the word that says yes. A word that's at home without a home

Here: synonym of cats, the common name of Isha and Haya

Here:

How happy we have been

How unhappy we have been

How we are ——————

In the end, we will have been ——————

Why it is good to write in French: the language in which the palindrome *Ici* exists

Into this miraculous Notebook comes the idea to open a little notebook of the Big Little Terrors perhaps at the back of this notebook turned upside down. Yes? No?

E.g.: Big Little Terror at 8 a.m. this morning 28 March: after a long interlude as delicious and deep as a living book, a treasury of memories cultivated à deux, suddenly: Nana on fire. Fever, flames, fucked. Declares having felt frail and feverish upon waking. In a trice the golden time is upended, demolished in a groan. Enter fear. H says: Doliprane. Or sesame. Or another such formula. Ten minutes later fever quashed. Is it the power of the word, of love, of faith, of suggestion, of conjuration? Where does the pharmakon reside? Report: Nana is struck by a sudden sore throat at the top of the Allée Fustel de Coulanges at the level of No. 33, sensation of suffocation, eruption of ganglions under her chin. In the space of three minutes H is spinning in terror's dance of death. The night of the 28–29th haunted, wild dance, atrocious playlet, rhythm: out of a silent Chaplin film, Nana gives up the ghost, Nana at the age of two goes off all by herself to see the Ocean, Nana found, burial of Nana, H falls into the grave with Eve and Nana behind a wall of wood, Pif pulls Eve out of the hole, H says: Wait! What are you doing here? This is all a nightmare, H outside Nana's room closed door, uninterpretable little high-pitched squeaks, 6 a.m. Nana's

room closed, not a breath, door indecipherable, 7:10 a.m. silence.
—Silence

Silence

What If?

H prowls around Silence's door, stabbing pains in her chest.

Sudden charge of a regiment of terrifying scenes: H sees H enter. Nana motionless. Nana's beautiful shining visages shone in the Allée Fustel de Coulanges, shone, shine in silence in the whole of her mental room

H desires passionately to leave this world.

Nana's breathing is H's whole heart and blood, of all beloved daughters the daughter best beloved. The life of H: at a standstill. The cats do triple flips. H puts off reflecting upon the most tragical tragedy until Later.

H goes out. Unruly flight of terrors accompanied by disgusting black buzzings in the white staircase. The door opens. Nana appears in Eve's dressing gown, the pastel-pink one, smiling. Rout of the regiment all the very powerful phantasms fade away, burial on the spot of the burial, a fraction of a second ago their troupe occupied all of reality

Song of the cuckoo

Contagions

If Nana lungs are burning

H feels her lungs burning

If H burns with Nana's burning, with what burning does Nana burn?

Ask your mirror-neurons, says Pif.

H feels her way from thought to thought: my mirrors don't mirror don't mime anyone but me.

Who in place of Nana, of cats in their robes of vair, of Eve, of the much beloved, of Pif, my chosen mirrors, do they reflect?

As if there were among my selves king or queen or king-queen or maybe a crystal throne variously occupied and shimmering

The door: I open. What are you waiting for?

H: Nana terrifies me

Nana: Sorry! Sorry!

H: Not your fault. I blame it on my imagination, devastated since the 1948 attack, ablation of my father without anaesthesia, ever since riddled with holes, mended, unrepaired, skin porous until death

'Nana,' name of the life-that-I-can-lose

It was in the *Unheimlich* time when the space between Here and There had been brutally extended

The streets, oh how disquieting they were, turned virtual as if designed by computers, yet we'd been going up and down them unwarily for decades, all of a sudden they can no longer be trusted—

I have a street problem, H says, I don't recognize them, it's as if they accuse me, they are everywhere, I am denounced

H is stuck in 'habitual' 'reality' with yesterday's brain, like someone who doesn't want to be born, all of a sudden expelled, delivered into an unreal reality, as in one of Poe's extraordinary tales turned ordinary, incontestably, as if it was at the door and there was no door, no entry

Monday, 30 March: 'nothing to report.' This 'Nothing' overwhelms me. Here, too, as in the Weddell Sea, here is the *Endurance*, first battle with the impenetrable barrier they seem to spy open water in the offing, it's a hallucination, they push onward, they think they are moving, nothing happens, the green sea suddenly turns indigo, they advance slowly, on the spot, nothing to report, H with anxiety watches for any sign of change in the wind, in the weather, at 7 a.m. it is 3 a.m. or vice versa

where is Here? It is here on page 13Ka of Notebook I, at the same moment on the other (notebook, ship, hill) already at sun-up it is unbearably hot, you'd think the sky was on the side of the pestilence, we need a company of the like-minded, Thucydides thinks, no distractions, quite the contrary we wish to stay close to the epidemic, but as it happened once, long ago, 2,400 years ago, as it will be 2,400 years from now, the war is right here, it is always war, here is the war on the war, now as it will be 2,400 years from now,

The days when there is 'nothing to report,' are days for the historians, homage to the doctor priests of the human condition moved by their 'duty' to bear witness, that strange impulse of the soul, the urge to paint life in the midst of the forces of death, this day nothing to report, only 2,400 dead, the living have their moment, turn yellow, drop, already a tender, translucent foliage grows towards the light

Nothing strikes me more than those very rare events of the Eventless that come to our attention via their tenuousness amid the flood of explosions registered non-stop in the scrupulous accounts of Battles at least as tragic as those of Stalingrad, ceaselessly pounded bombarded machine-gunned between Tuesday, 10 November 1942, and Wednesday, 3 February 1943, attacked 83 times, lacerated, the Don and the Volga overflowing with cadavers, save for the three periods when violent death takes 15 minutes off for a sandwich before re-launching the butchery, how to write this Nothing, this lightning-quick Gap between Charybdis and Scylla, time to howl the two names of the bi-monster, this day between the earth solitude and chaos and the shadows, before the day before the night just before the name and the death, that is nameless, and which can sometimes requires 86 attacks to declare victory.

Today, in the midst of the Nothingness, is the day of the battle between 'Literature' and King Pestilence

'Literature' suffers high losses, fends off attacks, distinguishes itself during skirmishes, without regaining any terrain. Increasingly H resorts to diversionary tactics. Notes the dandelions of daily life. Tufts of yellow pierce the asphalt. Small-scale flowerings, lively and humble.

Not the least desire 'to write a book' and no regret for not feeling the least desire.

Humility of the book: 'I am privileged, a creature of luxury, an aristocrat toying with time, a self with means, a self totally overwhelmed by the grandeur, the extent and democratic inventiveness of the plague. A bestseller sort of misfortune, misfortune of an entire country, and even of the whole world.

Tuesday, 31 March, Day of the First Chagrin, Isha opens her mouth wide Isha utters cries shrill as a whistle from the foot of the stairs, she addresses the whistles blasts at H. Her mouth yawns open and she howls. Howls with all her might. The stairs are steep, the sound rises. H struck notices nonetheless the prettiness of the narrow mouth with its pink tongue. Isha mouth remains open. The howl goes on and on, it is more than a match for the indifferent mountains it climbs walls as if its passionate little soul were ready to give up the ghost

to life's cruelty

never before has anyone so weaponized the cry. *Alas, what good?* A young woman, battling terrible pain, unable to give birth to a furious howl, how high enormous and dark and deaf are the mountains, so long as the pain goes on you howl like a fire alarm like an American ambulance, to frighten the pain, frighten H, or the fire alarm, and in vain, what good bursting a vein?

She no longer addresses anyone, the howl measures itself against nothingness, defies injustice's darkness, her smallness is immense, she carries her suffering further than human imagination, the human is mute, H is reduced, withered, she sees the stunted pettiness of her helplessness in the mirror the howl rises proud as a flame,

How is this going to end? It won't. It will end too late.

H seeks help, an extinguisher, an idea, staggers, poor echo of real suffering, poor in kindness, poor in genius why doesn't she find? The howl continues, why? why? Oh! Here comes Eve's dying cry again: why why?

What why? Why death? Why not death? Why must life die? Why?

H finds a little doorstop on the landing at the foot of the coat rack. This simulacrum of a dead mouse, of a top, works like a charm to staunch the wound and stop the howling. Isha pounces on the distraction. H is exhausted by the anxiety the scene has caused. Roland is dead. Help arrives as foretold by the law of life: too late. In the end it is too late. There are no more hours. No seconds. Time is empty

H has understood the message. That deep-black cloud is called: I want to go 'outside-in-the-garden-with-the blackbirds-where I have never been.' I was born free. Don't kill my birth. Don't lock me up. Hear my blood's urgency. I already sense that I don't know. I know all I'll ever know. Open and admit: am I not a cat? Don't you know I know that you know?

V

THE HOUSE WAS A BOOK

The House was a book. It took place at many different times and on several floors at once. Today was Saturday, 27 June. The House was exactly like Shackleton's *Endurance*, built to endure in all circumstances and perils, in fire and in ice.

H herself had built it in 1960 during Hurricane No. 1. The unimagined violence of the 60s had thrust her out of her usual story and onto an unknown continent: this was the first shipwreck. The tornado spins you round as in a soup of darkness, you thinkthinkthink this is it this is the end, and suddenly the atoms that constitute you discover that they are in the first hours of what will become My Story.

That's when I dreamt this dream: first of all, I discovered the walls of the Space were made of millions of ants, plunging me into glacial terror. Later you realize that was the initial Chaos. Then there's a door, my cats, my heart's delight, arrived in a car, leapt into the room emptied of ants right down to the last leg, crossed the scene's geometry and made for the balcony with the greenest and most familiar things. I had just watered. Lovely Isha pounced on a large pot with its dormant rose bush and began to drink. Water mixed with dirt. That's when, in a fraction of a second, she launched herself into infinite Openness (she was gone before I noticed) onto the top of a fence and up there, beyond the reality principle, propelled by the call of pleasure, wingless, body led by her lovely queen of Antiquity head, I see that she is about to walk on air, swept along by desire's crazy strength and nothing else, as gods once walked on water. Beyond, as far as the eye could see, oceans of empty air. The void all around. (This time I foresaw what the next half-second would bring. The sharp claw of its imminence pierced my heart. I uttered a great terror-filled cry. The cry saved us: its point pierced the dream's skin and it burst with the silence of a soap bubble. Such piercing cries are super-sounds sheer and steely as white silks, like supersonic crystals, imperceptible to the ordinary ear, but audible to entranced humans under certain extra-human circumstances, like the voice of God calling himself on the prophet's internal telephone.)

Later it comes to me that it is on the planet's pinnacle, a millimetre from nothingness, when all that remains of the world is a narrow ribbon where only a cat, thanks to its superhuman gifts, can fit, when life teeters on the edge not knowing which side it is on, when still alive you are already dead and dead you still live, in this eyeblink whose duration, however, is infinite, I tell myself, that the chosen may hear the Voice (of) God.

The voice is a whistle, the sum of all God's languages, whose timbre is instantly transmitted in the chosen one's language. Naturally at that moment, the chosen is not aware he's been chosen, he knows nothing, he is almost not, his whole being is the tympanum designed to receive God's whistleword. What God says is immense but can be summed up, on paper, by a modest all-powerful message: 'Here I am' or even simply: yes yes. In other words: Yes, you are living. Signed: Gods (plural).

That said, I add, I translate, I could roll out a tale, paint a steep, rugged landscape, unchain a storm, etc. But in His Truth the God(s) breathes in monosyllables. It's a language with one-word-and-one word, a yes-word in a repertory of endless music.

And just before being cast from life's uttermost point into the void, the soul balks, you are jerked awake on this side, this one, this one where there are tribes and populations, words by the billions, swarms. Slowly someone raises an eyelid. Someone takes the edges of day in their hands, pulls, opens, while the other, nocturnal life seeps away, and someone says (or thinks): I. At this moment, the moment when you say 'day is breaking'— the being who thinks (or says) 'I' is as big as the Earth, or bigger: 'I' could begin to conjure up the planet and what surrounds it.

Except with the cats, who reign over the present Moment, I was mostly in the third person, at an undecidable distance from myself.

I was *in* the house as a character is in a book. I often saw this third person go downstairs, prompted by some worry or other, always the same dilemma, she would like to be in one bound at the foot of the stairs, and the next second race to help those at risk, the list of whom kept her on the alert (cats, mother, squirrel, mouse, the 'vulnerable', the excluded and banished of all nationalities . . .) but she went down wary of the comblanchien stairs that one after another bared their teeth at her.

From the time of its construction, the Stairs of the House were dedicated to Descent. It is a staircase to the depths. As the interior's most important single element, it permits and invigilates all the moves of the unconscious. There one falls, drills, pierces, rummages, discovers, communicates with the descendances and the correspondescendances.

The Staircase is inevitable.

The meaning of 'comblanchien stairs' has been the same from the first, the 1961 descent to the first descent of Sunday, 28 June 2020, a rapid passage through the staircase's white cage, slender as a fine coffin, upright in its character and haunted by the fear of falling. In her arms, the creature with whose survival she has been entrusted, and it is precisely this mission that makes her tremble, makes her both guardian and traitor. The stairwell with its white teeth is her private version of Isaac's assassination by his father-who-loves-him. Everything has and will always happen as if it were a rehearsal for the first time, when the Vision flung its flames in her face while she was descending the stairs with her infant son like Virgil clutching

Dante to his breast to cross a stair the size of a human foot on the flank of the infernal Himalayas, the first time was the secret repetition of a first time lost in the depths of another memory in another time in another house. But in Virgil's case he trembled not a whit more than a Tibetan, it was Dante who trembled violently, whereas in her case it was the parent who'd have howled with fear had there been someone to hear, but there was only her, that is me, and the howls evaporated into the unmoving mineral whiteness of the stairwell where the icy stairs unfolded one by one

No one escapes such a trial unscathed. And even had a six-decades-long torrent rushed down the scene of the event without changing or exhausting its freshness, the murderous hypothesis neither aged nor retreated. A murder had taken place, in a prehistoric region someone had killed someone they loved, impossible to comprehend how or why that violence and cruelty were tied to love. Such was the law of the mythological staircase, the warning it uttered as soon as she set her toe on the top step. The ritual irruption of malice into love. Love and assassination conjoined.

The staircase never changed; its limestone stairs rippled like an icebound sea, its geometry of fearsome passions, its enigmatic monument demanded that she question the significance of this *palpable*, disquieting presence. No one is meant to ignore death, it builds its iron nest in the body's crux.

Now the nurseling was 60 years old and nothing had changed, she opened her eyes before daylight, to flee death she opened the door, the cats, two streaks of light, leapt, she took one step and the Staircase began. The Staircase hadn't aged. Such is its white marble nature.

Then, by surprise, I took a dream on the right, it was a dream of flight: in order to traverse the City with Omi—

Omi the abridgement of allmothers of whom I am the latest, when she appears it's because of all the figures of my-mother-in-a-dream, it was always Omi my German grand-mother who seemed most likely-to-flee in the least promising and most desperate manner: Omi, the smallest of women, tries her best to run but her short legs slow her down, how would she escape the Nazi horde without me and the hand I hold out to her ever since the streets of Oran, I haul her along Arzew Street, from Osnabrück to Africa the smell of sulfur pursues us, I am five years old and I understand that this is my lot: to tug-drag Omi out of the fangs' reach—

I suggested we walk along the Cemetery. Nobody is there, I tell myself, we avoid danger, the contamination: we march straight ahead, no stoplights. But I'm sorry, Omi, if you don't like going by the tombs. Escape death with the help of the dead is my brainchild. For you, it's in bad taste. However, we won't go through the middle of the tombs, only along one side, on the path that skirts the field of the mute

when night comes

now we are asleep the two of us in the big bed that is the dream's only piece of furniture. Then, all of a sudden, 'they' bang on the door. Above all, let's not answer, let's not budge. Isn't the door locked tight? The Nazis rattle it. Silence. Finally, they seem to have given up.

In a dream, when death comes, I sometimes burst the dream with the help of a *rending cry*, sometimes I wrap myself in silence, I don't budge, lying on the Bed by my mother I play dead I was already reduced to nothing, I say.

Even in 2020 the Nazis tracked us down, they came from the depths, shadows on the march in the shadows, I've never seen them face to face, by daylight, with faces, it's always the horde, organized, panting, tireless, pursuers all melted into one fearsome beast, the multiple dragon from the time before time, updated with a modern logo, never will I be able efface them once and for all, I tell my son, piling Asias and Africas between us and them is useless, they cross, they are transmitted and retransmitted through Omi's skin,

And it was she herself who had built the House, shaped its body with its narrow hips around the spinal column of the comblanchien and not one of its inhabitants has escaped its cold geometry, since 1960 we've lived in the Book, its well of light, its sides, its coldness, its black bars aglitter like an armoury full of lances and still today I hadn't clicked that the body's form was that of Montaigne's Tower with its library under the skull, she herself lived in the eaves with her books at chest level

I see myself seeking to tame the Staircase, says my sound physicist son, the Staircase speaks to me through clenched teeth, it threatens, it promises blood, I see my fall, the crack in my skull the curtain of blood, head bandaged for weeks—I'd warned you and it happened, had you listened to me, Caesar, but no one ever heeds the warning of an errant poet

Death of a mouse

From the book-populated heights I see myself at the window waiting for the postman. The postman is the god of the outside world. All the computers past and to come will never abolish this Messenger who comes from the shores of the Scamander from the shores of the Yangtze from the shores of Lethe carrying coals and embers, I tell myself. The House, thus the Tower, is constructed *in anticipation of the postman*, it is a lookout, the idea of the postman has shaped the interior which is squat, turned taut towards what is to come, Isha keeps watch beside me, her body thinks: Only danger can come from the infinite beyond, let's prepare for the onslaught. Keeping watch beside Isha, Haya thinks: Let's prepare a feast for the enemy, war or peace, we're prepared. What's going to happen to us, our thoughts I wonder, crouched behind the books. I stand between inside and outside, she, H, vacillating, thinks from the paper-thin junction of two universes fine as the membrane that does not separate night from its day,

she is drawn by what she fears, fascinated by what in fleeing she prepares to receive.

Meanwhile, I observe these states of incarnation and I make a note of them, as a painter on the beach with his vibrant brush chases the quick-moving clouds, as touch by touch the water changes colour and timbre, one would need, I tell myself, to be an orchestra with a hundred vibrant brushes, what am I saying, four hundred to render this moment's *la*, and

At that very moment, like a metaphor improvised on the spot for the great secret theatre of the Anthropocene, a Mystery with a sacrifice suddenly unfolds on the garden's sandy stage. As always in a show of this sort, it is the victim's last hours. The audience is me. The victim her, the eternal mouse

The audience thinks: chance assigns me the role of witness. I am a guest at the tragedy. I have nothing to do with it. An old, old play in the garden. My role is to be powerless: the strange, quietly violent ballet of Haya and the mouse makes me death's acolyte. The two partners are as beautiful as lovers drunk on seduction. There is a pursuit, halt, pursuit, defeat, relaunch, arousal of desire by terror, life fired up by death's caress, you see quickly that the dancers are unable to release one another, blood-ied, they run. The cat is a big silky mouse, a Chinese acrobat, a youthful trapezist who smiles at the abyss, the mouse is a micro-cat with supercat speed, she doesn't run she flies. This is love: nothing more deliciously suicidal than desire. Follow me, flee me, miss me, lick me go.

The mouse doesn't try to escape. She could. She cannot. She is spellbound. She can't leave the cat alone. The cat could let the mouse go. The cat lets go. Savours a moment of boredom. Lights a cigarette. Or a cigarillo. So this is how it is, thinks the mouse. Is it a game? The mouse stops moving. She reflects. In her linden robe, one might imagine an oak or arbutus tree. She looks more and more like a dead leaf. She grows bigger. Her four warm centimetres fill the frame.

Where is she, the cat asks. I don't know either, I say. The game was

endless, I was enjoying myself. We felt fear, we felt desire, for the heart it was a test of endurance, there was no malice, we thought we would die, maybe we did—is she under some foliage, waiting for the postman to tell her what to do? By dint of running, of fleeing, of hiding, she has become extraordinary. Humanity, in sum. Her tail is like a strand of thread

And she was waiting for the postman. Condemned? Or saved, given back to the light, to the forest's generosity, to the Ocean's gift? Or saved for another day?

She was waiting for the verdict.

It wasn't 'the postman' she was waiting for, it was:

life or its refusal

the battle's outcome. The battle unfolded like all battles on the other continent

the Letter

the Transfusion

the last minute.

He had said I'll call you in five minutes. And ever since she's been waiting for the fifth minute. The first four minutes ticked by according to the rhythm of her watch and since then she's been waiting for the fifth. Or was it the fifth minute whose seconds were growing slower and slower? Or time wandered off at the beginning of the fifth minute, and History seemed to be stopped in the middle of a chapter, like a lazy river

she was waiting for the postman to come and fix it

Around the clock you could count on the postman

To deliver the paper meals that nourished the box

But he didn't tell, his words were sealed

Give, the postman didn't do that,

He promised, he passed on the secrets, but only in passing

Tragedy's understudy

The one who comes and knows not and for naught

The cruel, ignorant, innocent messiah

A traveller from distant lands, who comes in passing, who passes on

For a hundred years the same postman

Understudy for permanence in the absence of permanence

His name? Postman.

Almost the same since the days of the stable

Considerable had begun in 1298, in response to a need of Marco Polo's

Always dressed in the same practical outfit, all that has changed is

His mount,

Nowadays the postman came on a motorbike,

Hers at least, her personal courier; and it is now in the postman story, after sixty long years of waiting, that the first change occurred: she no longer heard the postman cross the invisible distance, finished the buzz of wings stirring space some two kilometres from the House, vroom-vrooming like an earthbound airplane, the long thread of the wait was cut, henceforth the delivery person came without warning the way a carp rises silently through the water's thicknesses, the bike's lips are sealed

thus, much of the postman panoply no longer exists, I thought,

never again will I hear him crossing the earth; there are still such things as letters but the species is endangered, I'll try to disappear before it does, I tell myself, there's still the word *post*, and its countless relays and riders still travel the roads of my mental post office. Horses die in the end, but the letters mailed from London in 1588 continue to arrive from across continents at the House that is my beacon over the ocean of lands

What makes the House's beauty so touching: one *sees* the postman arrive, suddenly there he is at the end of the nocturnal buzz, cockcrow, you'd think, and his image in his red- and-yellow plumage signifies: I am putting the world in the box for you

Back in the 60s, the deaths, the plagues, executions of firstborns, all sorts of calamities promised by the Bible happened in the House, outside in front of the House, wars camped, they killed died massacred buried banished raped lands and seas and the trees grew their screen in front of her and her tower of paper

The postman put the message in the same box: this was a play by Shakespeare whose first word was *Now*

Maintenant

She preferred the French word *Maintenant*. The word *Now* frightened her like an order to kill, like the barking of a wolf, that was why she loved it, out of her love of fear. But she preferred the rich, contradictory hours of *Maintenant*. This was a name for the mystery that offered her what it concealed from her, that sharply withheld what it held out to her. And in this instant called 'maintenant' that fluttered overhead, very close and yet as far above her as the fairytale airplane, the twentieth century's gift to Marcel Proust, a palpitation, that beat its delicately veined transparent wings, that didn't land, that soared, granted a wish and was eclipsed, she felt she received the caress of an eternally offered hand, giving itself on 22 May 1976 for eternity, dumb with intimidated ecstasy she felt the adored hand murmur—so very silently like the language in a dream—the speech of eternity, she thought: it is this discourse of hand to hand, this hand-givingness that, in the absence of a name, one calls 'god', a sensual sensation of transcendence, a dizziness of the self suddenly lifted far beyond the body's coffer, and no longer connected with a place (a divan, a chamber) save the place of the hand under the giving given hand, overwhelmed, I can still feel your hand alight, settle on my hand like an eagle in heat, your square palm, the astonishingly soft skin, closed eyes— for your hand was a face abandoned on the face of my hand— your secret soul overflowing onto my fingers onto the ravished page of my palm, in a state of absolute spiritual freedom, freed from the laws of society, from the conditions of the sojourn in reality, since all this occurred in the infinite regions of grace, a species of dream that is a grand awakening, absolved of lies, of error, of limit, of condition, of qualification, of the service of truth, of justification, unsullied by commentary or excuse

Whoever were to glance at my hand would see it coated in this golden ointment

that invisible ink that Poe describes so meticulously in his story 'The Gold-Bug', the inscription illegible to the undiscerning eye, that dazzles anyone susceptible to the manifestations of the secret. I myself have the rare and blessed surprise to feel, suddenly, the lightest of frissons, almost a tingling, from my wrist to my fingertips, as if the ghost of a bird settled, beat its wings and flew off again. I look at my hand, time has printed hundreds of wrinkles on it, but the supple firmness, the silky assurance of your hand has not changed

A few instants later, He said in the calculated, prudent voice he used to weigh his words: 'I will-always-find-us-a present.'

She thought: to find a present in the present that is never present, one must start by thinking of thinking about it

It was the afternoon of 22 May 1976, they were seated on the divan in the study, in the distance Time's Ocean was lowing was absorbing the weight of a hand given for ever, and in her hand an impalpable and calming love was being diffused

When we are ninety, he would utter these words, his phrase and his

prayer when he opened his eyes after love, slowly and with precaution returning from a long voyage, not yet moving, oh no, not before assuring himself that he was coming back to a flat world, no abysses, no violent strangeness, no eternities, like someone who has fainted, who comes back warily and almost incredulously from a stay in theory reserved for the dead or the rapt. He must have had the sensation of a brief death, round trip guaranteed, from which he had to surface as fast as possible, dripping, saddened, for a salvation with the taste of an adieu.

Then he would say: When we are ninety! You might think that this future was the future promised. But the voice's timbre groaned. But it was the future of a splendid impossibility. Of that golden age we had the aura, the dazzlement as in a dream that had almost no chance of coming true. And this *almost*, he invoked it in a soft, shy voice, respectful of fatality.

For a few seconds he almost possessed this bliss. He will have had its premonition, I tell myself. Now and then one can almost possess what one does not have I tell my daughter.

That is what the House was for. Beneath its solid, reassuring and modest aspect, all qualities it takes from my mother, it served as a temple. It was on one of its walls whose secrets she kept that he had inscribed these words:

Ich bin hier and today

And it is here and today that you are day after day

'I am here

    and today'

my daughter says—Can you say that?

Sacreative, I say.

Creates something ungrammatical, my daughter says

Sacred, say I.

It's as if you were to say: I am the today

Precisely, say I.

It is a performative phrase that proclaims the presence of the subject of the

    enunciation. The subject is only there when he says 'I', my daughter says.

I watched him stand facing the wall, writing as if the wall were dictating its

    hardness, murmuring its tomblike duration, I say

He was the today

From the point of view of the death of the dead person there is no 'day', my

    daughter says.

From the point of view of the dead person *today* is all that exists, I say

There is no more presence of the present, my daughter says

I thought: I am face to face with love's mystery

The cats bustled about, never far from each other, loping off and coming

back, disappearing so as to get back together, lost and found again, apart so as to call each other,

rehearsing love's mystery and the death of death

in love

Haya! Isha! I called the cats, they answered: Here I am! in their language,

They called: Haya! Isha! Each in our language we called and answered, if I called: Philia! Aletheia! right away my former cats appeared on the gravel walk

I am here

and today

murmured the choir

A hallucination perhaps but as apparition it possessed a more intense and satisfying reality than vision's so-called exterior reality

Love keeps the dead alive, on condition, of course, that the love is of good quality—especially the cats.

Between the cats of old and the cats of now, no bad feelings, no decay of love.

Cats don't have ghosts, I tell my daughter, they trust to memory in order to persist in peace. Time does not fade their bodies. There is a marvellous fidelity

Now he was ninety, of which seventy-five alive and fifteen dead,

Now, ninety, that age of Cockaigne, that promised season, you are there, I thought.

It was the day of one of our anniversaries, 25 June, one that goes back to the year 2020, I was trying to put some order in time's disorder, to give a form to the fusion of our times with Time and the times. In time's floating domain, all that lives is endlessly being stirred up, hallucinated, deracinated, derallucinated, nothing stays the same, measurements are forever being exceeded, take forty years of life, twenty years ago they counted for a hundred, today the same ones count for twenty, you foresee the day they will count for ten. What frightens me, I was thinking, is the idea that in a few year-units, the same forty years of life might be overtaken by as many years of death, at that point, we would have lived together nearly eighty years, half of them dead. Anything can happen to us, youths, old ages, immortalities, rebeginnings,

what is no longer what it has been is even more, His thought said

the past passes in front of the House, it hasn't changed, it doesn't change,

the house retains, retains us perpetually, us and our anxieties about disappearing.

The Now, the *Maintenant* is this hand, the *main* you give me to hold even when you are not here

I look at my right hand. There, between the fingers, is where your hand settled once and for all in 1976 after the deluge; since then they have never been apart

Sometimes she opened her hand and felt the invisible and magic presence of time's hand in hers, this might happen, her right hand contained some of the *now*, some of the *maintenant*, the hand that pecked at the page with the beak of the pen, the hand the beloved hand had settled upon, depositing an inexhaustible store of *nows*. This could happen. In 2020 as in 1976.

Now she was twenty-seven, she was on her way to America where one of her Lives' many cantos was waiting for her, at the end of this Life filled with elements borrowed from the Odyssey, from the books of the Kings, and especially from the spirit of the adoring Gilgamesh, student of death and its dangers, she came back to the House. Her Life in the Other World didn't follow her.

After a few years she went on [elle *parcheminait*] and became a story as spectral as dry leaves in an herbarium. She had been. Later she would wonder who that person she had long ago ceased to be was, that person she didn't really understand, who had gone about under another name, whom she never now encountered: someone who had incontestably been the subject of one of her existences, who had no attachment to the cats or to writing. If she came across her today, would she recognize her? She reminds me of those personas whom a character like Moll Flanders or Roxana successively inhabits, those adventurers in the Life of a Woman who owe their various existences to that pioneer of literary transgenres the man-woman Daniel Defoe, I tell myself. I have almost nothing in common with them, save for the House, the birthplace, with its lookout whence I keep an eye out for the postman or the world, as other incarnations at other times have done.

In this *now*, she was seventy-five years old with her mother beside her, slowly she descended the Staircase, it was Eve her mother descending, each of us thinking as we descend Ourstory's last stairs, our bodies are changed—who cares the hearts think, nothing has changed, we still feel and are attuned, our hair is white, wrinkles crease our cheeks but the laughter rings out in Time's face, each day is succulent, I held my mother's hand, my mother's arm, I bore her astride my back, she grew thinner and thinner, she grew heavier and heavier, what with the weight of life-and-yes, Eve said, you may well weigh less, still you are heavier and heavier.

I am ephemeral, my mother says, my voice is cracked, I recall during the war we had to bring the nails for Hindenburg, which war? Afterward Hindenburg had vanished, afterward it was war, war after war, each war *the* war, it's funny how short life is, there's not much time between the wars, I haven't forgotten, her rusty little voice says, I was never an ace in the memory department but when the French arrived, it was the cavalry with horses, in Strasbourg not Osnabrück, Place de la République, later it was Place de l'Empereur Nicolas or someone, later it was the Place d'Armes, the buildings had a window low down, we stood there and watched the French go by, later the

Americans, Kaiserplatz yet another emperor, Omi and I were
in the Contades Garden around the park, it was paved, a football
hit my sister in the chest and she couldn't breathe, I still hear
Omi shouting at the soldiers. Later my son also got run over on
the Square. I cried with the Americans. At school we were the
little German girls in calico—calico, do you know that word?—
all of a sudden it became a French lyçée and who came? Little
French girls in ringlets and short skirts

What a lovely trip to Strasbourg we're having, I think,
keeping a firm hand on the metal railing, always the Fall waits
for us, like all Strasbourg trips, each trip accompanied by the
shadow of the previous one, the Square keeps some secret, in
my opinion it's the Cathedral with the Synagogue with its
broken arm, my mother like the cicada that just yesterday was
Pythia with her cane and the cathedral also, the Strasbourg
cane, from one cane to the next cane

I say: Act I: the past. Act IV: the present. Eve-my-mother
says: there is no such thing. War after war, tomorrow and tomorrow and the present. It's complicated

How we get from the bedroom to the Strasbourg table to
New York where Eve and Eri take the subway to visit the cousin
who adopted one of her deported older sister's two children,
one does what one can, near Central Park, therefore we are in
1980, I say did they take the boy or the girl? In 1945 the stories
are brightly coloured but all mixed up, with three steps to go
before the bottom she stops, lost,

Where are we? my mother squeaks. In 2012, I say. Already!
my mother laments. She has the high-pitched voice of a mouse

She was going down the stairs, what was always present, she was thinking, was Shakespeare, mama and the beloved, and also Homer, and also the whole agitated, populous library, teeming, bountiful, all those beings that all of a sudden thrust themselves from the crowd, or rose up at the call of a word, a melody, a code, a numeral, or didn't respond at all, resisting the temptation of simultaneity. One cannot be multiple all the time, only now and then, out of concern for the truth, from scrupulosity, not enthusiasm.

Thus (at this very moment which flashes like a fish under my hull so quick it is pointless to give it a date) I have just written-thought this question: Who'd have believed that yesterday evening she might have been in China—on the misty border where the mountain belongs perhaps to India, in the narrow, glacial place where the fire of a great battle was being kindled, and the start of this fire was so small, an immense calamity all of a sudden flared up in a tuft of frozen grass between two stones in the Himalayas, add a few soldiers, a handful of enemy brothers, three insulting gestures and everything is ablaze, the mystery of the world-wide outbreak, the violent death of a planet,

But who remembers the 1962 Sino-Indian War? Until last Monday she herself had forgotten it, didn't remember the same war in 1922, nor any another, nor even her personal wars, and massacres, and hates, and look how the eruptions, earthquakes, grasshopper invasions, epidemics turned up, sometimes with a half-century of delay sometimes with hundreds of years of delay, memory was a pestilence she tried to visit as seldom as possible. Not remember was not to forget, it was like writing the History of the Post Office, mail a letter from the end of the world in 1298 or in 1998 and let it wander from post to post, stopping off here and there to be an eye witness, trying to decipher the sense of the things of this world, the way an astronomer studies the world of the stars so as to slowly decipher its laws.

Time was a land as oft visited as the sky

It is only now that the year 1962 was revealed to her mind in the Staircase

1962

The postman brought me a letter sent by Eve-Cixous-mid-wife from Barberousse prison. The letter said: mind the lemons in the icebox, they're the hen that lays the golden eggs. I eat well at lunch couscous and yogurt for dessert. You can't say we are afraid. I'm reading Camus's *La Poste*. After *Père Goriot* I've slipped a notch or two. I'm stunned by the doctor who didn't right away diagnose cholera, there were so many people who died in 1940 but your father wasn't allowed to practice medicine. So many rats it's terrible it wasn't funny all those people who were rats or mice. But I keep an open mind. Who'd have thought that today I'd be writing you from the women's prison? And no rats

So there was writing paper in prison

Now, I was thinking, here I am and no Eve on my back. In May 1962 it's her broad firm foot that presses on my heart,

When she was in prison I couldn't breathe, my chest crushed under the weight of Barberousse fort, under that no-exit monument, stopped dead, petrified, totally memoryless, actionless and actless, eventless, senseless, the House mimicked a prison, I stopped moving, all travel suppressed, thought arrested,

it's only now, sixty years later, that 1962 turns up, more distant than Algiers' Casbah,

62, in the stairs of the Casbah, is the number of the Incarceration. Eve is fifty-two, she's enjoying herself in there with the locked-up, among thieves and prostitutes you are in good company, finding the charms of women's liberation within prison walls is their secret, don't tell anyone there is comedy in the tragedy and adventure in literature's dungeons: all those letters in which you hide what you are saying, in which you disguise, deny, encrypt, wink—the games of the ladies who cheat at bridge or poker, subterfuge artists, are nothing compared to this game in which everything is signs, keys and double envelopes, where carrots, lemons, quotations, banalities are gold bugs. Don't tell a soul

Quick, I descend the last two stairs, Eve, now 102, squeaks chirps croaks, chuckles in survival mode on my back

Where are we?

Here, I say. We are here—here in 2012.

I set my mother down,

We can't go back, whirrs her crusty gay voice. When you want to survive you have to accept. Good luck! *Dank Gott für das!*

And I say: Act 4

It is funny life is short, chimes my mother. Just Monday I was watching the

soldiers play football and today? Last act!

With all these moments simultaneously putting forth shoots, wars that go on spreading, continental confusions, the House throbs like a woman in her ninth month, the page pants furiously and look, now she is ready to push.

These aren't memories, I was thinking, these are events of a particular sort, events that start at the same time like sudden little volcanic eruptions, you think your heart is withdrawn, a powerful illusion of armistice descends on the House, that's when

loud bangs at the door, the heart brutally aroused, the soul covered in a rain of ash and soot, did we forget death? The force of the perfidiousness, the explosion of the Unexpected within the Expected, a machine gun rat-a-tat-tat smack in the middle of Paradise

Overnight I lose Isha my life. She falls. Is crushed. I find her dead. I fear night. I'm afraid of the night. Dreams come. They accuse me. They stab me. They are utterly perfidious. They rerun. They haunt me. They denounce me. They lash out at my cats. Why the cats? Why the lambs?

Yesterday for the first time I was reunited with the troupe that plays the role of family in the chronicle of my life. We threw a party to celebrate our reunion. I walked into the room. It was full of people. A long, narrow gut-like room, so much for the place. Marie, my old classmate, wasn't there. Suddenly the thought of her death struck me, feeling her ghostly presence, I wept, my sorrow surprised me, I asked her to forgive me. Food was being served, fruit piled in pyramids. I stepped onto the balcony: so I was in Oran. So-and-so, a woman structurally depressed, leant over the railing, poised to plunge into the void, impelled by the obsessions that have troubled her since child-hood. When a woman dreams of falling, the dream commented, it's that she dreams of being a fallen woman, or that someone felled her. With a playful bound Isha-my-life perched on the arm hanging like a branch over the void. —Isha! I say—I was about to snatch her back when brusquely, brutally, the dream nurse grabbed the suicidal woman, yanked her back, provoking the catastrophe. She let go of Isha. I watched my beloved drop through the well of floors. Heart bleeding, unsteady, I raced downstairs. I reached the ground floor. I paused a moment before I entered the dream basement. I pulled up a few weeds before entering the dim recess that served as a storeroom for the unconscious, what in my childhood they called the ulterior motive.

Here I suspend my account for a few instants: it is the vagueness of my pause on the cellar's threshold that now, long after the event, attracts my attention, draws me precisely because just as I was removing a few weeds, gardening even, seriously, absent-mindedly, automatically, it was as if I was entranced, as if I'd suddenly lost sight of reality, as if reality switched off when I entered the basement, I remember that I felt nothing, experienced nothing, I was absorbed in the tufts of grass—weeds—this is the sort of thing you see in tales of bewitchment, in the Odyssey, in Grimm's fairy tales, all of a sudden, without your involvement, without warning, ordinary reason is kidnapped, there's a derailment but you were not alerted, and then, as if nothing had happened,

heart bleeding (here I pick up the story where I left off), I entered the dark place. One of the three Fates sat on the ground on the right, I think she cradled a small child. I saw nothing. I expected her to have picked Isha up, to be cradling Isha, injured, dying. Where is she? I ask. She points to the ground ahead of me on the left, in the dark alcove, a little package shrouded in a tea towel, Isha's body already abandoned, my beloved already separated from me, already a fleck of trash in the eternal bin, relegated to the infinite distance, extracted without anaesthesia from my heart, thus grief vomits its spasms far beyond the domain of language

While I am writing this story, hoping for a simple, faithful account, Isha my lovely, my grace, my song, my acrobatic irony, slips singing beneath my knees, she is safe and sound. Still, on my heart's left side, the pain of Isha-my-Life's death is slow to heal. Isha's death is fixed in my head like Berenice's teeth in the brain of Edgar Allen Poe.

I spend my time losing paradise, I tell my daughter.

18 April 2020, it was the day of the Game

Let's play I say. It is 18 April 2025. Do you recall the mornings the crows attacked? The virus cawed at the windows, the black dawns of 2020. I recall a young yesterday a school where I'm about to start school, outside in the streets the War caws, I am going to learn the alphabet, I think I am learning the language of birds, this is not a school, it is a noschool, the banished children repeat the notes o, i, o, i, we are in one of those 1940 Cities where the plague rules, the world is one great sore-infested country, constellations of slaughterhouses, each minotaur is allotted eight hundred thousand human beasts, amazed I repeat the notes, at the beginning of the Great University of the World I gather words that shine in the dark like pearls I say 'Krieg' like Omi my grandmother, I say 'Képi like my father the lieutenant, these are my first verbal treasures, at night the songster sirens howl their mythological howl, climb the magnificent octaves

103

I'm not able remember the days of 11 September 2001, was it 11 or was it 9? I don't hear the noise, mute images rise from the twisted columns of smoke

what remains unforgettable: I was watching TV. The television's cyclopian mouth gaped irresistibly. I thought: I am being swallowed up, this is an unheard-of event, I thought nothing, the bell tolled for us, all alone I watched us being buried alive, you were in China, the towers fell on us, don't ask for whom, my beloved telephoned, Look! This is our play's last scene, what time is it? The last hour

Of our world, I noted in my 2001 notebook, I could find it again

I thought. The thought machine has begun to think in all directions, it is under siege, panicked

You call me from Shanghai, saying: you are My China. We laugh, at that exact moment our towers crumple

And there you have it, instead of recalling the Plague Year 2420, I evoke 9/11. What remains: Ground Zero with you, you recite Donne's holy sonnet, this is our Monument, you say, we laugh, this is my play's last scene, it is here and today that my last scene is being played, you say, I don't laugh, you are speaking the truth and I don't believe you, and year after year I repeat the words of the world's last night,

This new plague, in the four corners of the planet, that is something you didn't imagine, my beloved little world

The year 2420 after Thucydides

The same day at the same moment the world signals: into great misfortunes small joys fall, chirrups in the distance; from her window my friend C sees blue sky, what does Moses see from his last window, never have we seen such a sky

In the Magenta District dirt and trash accumulate, a broken bathroom on the sidewalk, there'll be rats, there are rats, how many rats are there in the Ark of the arrival, in the overgrown garden a lone blind old woman has spoken to no one for two months nonetheless she wants to live

at the same moment in the forest the cuckoo throbs like the Song of the Earth: Life! Life! Such a small bird, from kilometres away you hear it

Acorns, I say, I am foraging acorns for the locked-up cats, it was the first day of spring, I imagine the eve of the opening of the Ark, the hullabaloo in its passengers' hearts, a pulsating orchestra the animals are panting, ready to die of happiness, during lockdown no one is born, all of us boxed up on time's waters; I hunt for acorns for the cats, it is too early in the season, I dream of opening the doors and letting them out. I am scared to open the doors. The temptation to give them Paradise and find Hell. They were born in the house's enclosure. They have not yet been born to the world. Haya plays under the bed with an unidentified object. The object is every-object. Haya gives it life, it mirrors life back to her, life of before-life. Down on her hands and knees H rummages under the bed for the Object.

When I go to our Carrefour supermarket, F says, the store is not clean, the employees are nice but dirty, I come out with the virus

in the street you notice people switching sidewalks, everyone crosses to the other side in the end the whole world finds itself on the same patch of pavement

What's the solution, my mother says. She who wishes to go far cares for her mount

The same day, that same Friday, two thousand four hundred and twenty without months it was perhaps another or still the same Thursday this damaged vanishing calendar, what they call the 'Robinson effect' time's debacle, here

Yet another day of pomp and circumstance—'Here,' the flying cats go up and down the tall spaces, *space* is an age in itself, the beloved says, they leap from century to century, install their landing strips here and there, multiply space by means of different levels

Cat edict

Doors are made to be opened. Celebration of openings. This House is full of doors: kitchen-cupboard doors: 9. Fridge door, linen-closet doors: 4, medicine-cabinet doors: 4, bedroom and living-room doors: 4, 4 and 3. From a human viewpoint these doors want to be closed, they set boundaries, mark fences, territories, separations, intimacies, multiply space, places to store secrets, interdictions, archives, tools. From the cats' viewpoint doors must not resist being open to their vital desire to go-and-see further, further, explore, give worlds to the world. Armoire door-door lessons: different ways to descend Eve's armoire via the North face. On the NW side by jumping from its summit to the narrow-as-a-path-on-one-flank-of-the-Himalayas shelf on the bedroom-door side, *if* the door is shut. If it's ajar, proceed to the armoire's other side. Glide between the scree of packages, cages, suitcases. Leap to the little round table landing beside the lamp, thence to the ground. All in three seconds

My daughter, my Nana contemplates the forest, it is 9 in the morning 2420

Good.

The word *good* warms H's heart like the first song of the first dove.

H—Good, what? Nana—The light.

As a peacock its tail, light shakes out its waves.

The Peace. The Quiet.

107

So that this nominal phrase, modest and sublime as the feelings of Felicity (Saint Francis of Assisi's great grandniece) may, over there in the depths of time whose corners one may only imagine, be seen emitting its soft, supernatural light under its cloak of banality it must don the crooked crown of its official date in the annals of the year 2420. We said that on Friday, 27 March, of this spring, a twin of the same Friday of that year in Athens when Thucydides wrote the first news story from the universal point of view in his Chronicles of Humankind. The noteworthy property of all these stories from No. 1 up to the story dated 2420: the repetition, so far unexplained, of the catastrophic mode, noteworthy for firing two shots in rapid succession: first the plague, then, right afterwards, the holocaust.

H and Nana were conscious of the great audacity of this sentence uttered without bravado and without humility. Good. No one, in fact, would hear these words. They were alone on the island of earth, a mother with her daughter and a daughter with her mother, with the squirrels in the oaks, high above time, and cats on the armoires, all of them off to the Poles.

What is extraordinary about this phrase is the unlikelihood that anyone could utter it on that day in the country of France to the numerous peoples assigned to one of the plagues of the biblical repertory on that day; the privileged admitted by unreadable chance to this timeless banality were very rare. What rendered the phrase even more extraordinary was its timeless banality, its tenuous, familiar message, and the fact that the privileged had no particular claim to this privilege. It was. One of Nature's microscopic causeless events. An aimless remark. We felt good. We were. Without date.

This was just after 30 March, some days previously it was 28 March. Such an extraordinary quantity of thoughts, events, windstorms and other anxieties had pressed,   like an army through a mountain pass, between those two March days that during the handful of instants Monday lasts, you'd never have time to report on the flood as it passed.

That same day, remember?

We discovered the presences and their forces, the forest's tenacious, slight but regular work, Week One, the march of the broom regiments, Week Two, the buttercup tapestry, Week Three, sheets of white rockrose stretched across the undergrowth, we were becoming botanists, we didn't know, it's natural, we came from the vegetable seas with their long, breaking waves of greens, crashing or foaming, and we hastened to look up the names of these phenomena, the mysterious orchestration of the yellows, golds, sonorous layers of scent, together we walked, the first to blaze a trail, nobody before us had had the good fortune or the need to meddle with the forest, with this co-memorial library as yet untouched by humankind, refined, harmoniously disorderly, with the first nations of pines, juvenile giants like my father, and their dead, totemized on the spot, sometimes scalped, slim young giants and the old ones moving together, chanting the long times of existence, a people persisting across the centuries of human time,

remember the Springtime Exposition? I remember the liberation chants of the unseen cocks, powerful voices awkward trumpets, ringing out in English: arise! arise! As if this was the voice after silence of the beloved on the phone, those forceful, triumphant notes, the bassoons and occasional drums of those peasant birds that provoke laughter among the birds of loftier spheres

constrained to silence from 1945 until March 2020 the birds, starting on 19 March, rushed into the long-forbidden air, no delays, no wavering, after the exodes, the exclusions, a diverse, multi-species people responds yes yes yes to the first call, vital as air and light, of this divinity we human aspirants call 'liberty'

Song of the cats:
    Down with ceilings
    Beyond the ceiling
    To the bottomless heights
    I'm a four-footed bird
    My mother's dream

Isha on the summit of the bookshelves, weighs, calculates, brooks no advice

In an instant her bound carries her to the summit

Even before the instant ends / To the heights of the heights / There is no way down / The wall is a vertical ceiling / Without asperities

I am Isha on the ridge, I wait for the ground to come and find me / Don't hurry down / For the descent / You must inverse-leap

I am Isha astride the invisible light

Independence is my flag

And the newspapers? The year was 2420. Above all no newspapers! These daily demons—easily exorcized dispersed the way Ulysses, in one breath, ejected the swarm of pretenders who had, for so long, infested the palace that the whole Ithaca world had finally dubbed as real and true the illusion that those fattened parasites were the natural masters of the nation

After a long usurpation a lightening expulsion

At first you don't hear the silence. One morning or evening you feel the almost imperceptible peace that shines where the old days brimmed with clatter and discord. A peace made of the deep, murmurous perfume spread by shoals of rockroses after a downpour, frail flowers that never stop dying and being born, die born, and are finally born.

And it rained. And the cats saw the waters spurt from the springs. And they ran to gather these narrow sparkling ribbons, this was the first time and they were struck with hundreds of cold, damp lines

Then Isha runs to me and lifting her face, her tiny mouth open, she calls: What is that? What is that? Rain, I say. It is Rain.

Isha: Rai/n! Rain/n, Haya! And Haya echoes: Rain! Isha says: Stop the rain! Stop

But the rain has no ears and doesn't heed the voice

Right here, enter Shackleton, thus: *then the fatal day dawned,*

And then nothing, a glacial aposiopesis, entry cut off, the day fatally gone with its fatality, we'll never know, it was a Sunday, sunk, he might as well have followed the Saturday 4 April Seminar that didn't take place, as the old calendars show,

Right here, the first sentence of a manuscript, perhaps the last, was found in a bottle,

the idea that literature's work consists in a battle with forests of sentences to reach the heart of language and drill a hole there to release the power of Silence

I imagine Silence like the Pole, pictured as a white and prodigiously tall rock on Mercator's projection of the world, and inversely like the irruption of white noise from the mine pits of language and their rumblings

here was a Sunday without a breath, once upon a time it would have followed a choral-seminar week, I would have gone on with the ancient, refreshed meditation that has been part of my inner life ever since I had installed in the 60s of some or other century, in my narrow cell of an apartment, a white box of an abode that a big bed almost entirely fills so it occurs to me that to counter the shut-in feeling I'm going to order a tall mirror on the internet in which I'll at least see myself, I'll verify I am there with me

only in jotting this dream down as testimony do I really see the extraordinary nature of this mirror in which I'll be head-to-toe reflected: first person, page, writing, last person. The mirror will give me the news

For me, the primitive, pole theme of everything I've tried to explore in my travels through time, the place and lair of the mysteries, the scene of fascination is: Prison. I'm utterly astonished. And its key words: encirclement, enclosure, incarceration, cloister, sequester, evasion, burial, resurrection, inside, Eve escapes, Peter Ibbetson,

and the word *boucler*: loop.

I've never been aware of the omnipresence of this theme, I know nothing of it I am in it, I am it, for me it is the bottle in which I

All the books I've ever wanted to reread, that is, read over and over compulsively, the books I've dived into as if lured by some bewitched and treasure-packed hole, finally I must admit they are all battlefields, thus accounts of sieges during which I am now besieged to the point of suffocation, extinction, even;

now the besieger as a book lays siege to its subject; now, stock still, for weeks on the lookout, months if need be with a cat's calculated, superhuman patience; now changing moods and tactics, harrying the besieged entity at some point designated as a point of weakness, and breaching it where I myself never expected to

Naturally I'm enticed by the books that resist, that defy the agonizing desire to Read, books that admirably delay the outcome with a series of tricks and detours, hoping against hope that there is no end at the end, that the siege will never be lifted, that the raft will see us through the floods, that the floods will not turn on us one night like a deluge bucket

It's not me who chooses these foreign bodies. My blood chooses, I read via transfusion.

This note of 5 April is reprised by the equally anguished note of 26 April as if the soul of the astonished child in me returns to throw herself against the same rock several times a season

In *Well-Kept Ruins* (a book I wrote Before the War, in a time as distant and present as the Trojan War, in which to write was the pleasure of making love with the dead), I said, accusing or pitying myself, that I alone among the people I loved hadn't been in prison in reality. Everyone else had been arrested and thrown in the clink at some or other moment but not me. On the other hand, each time I was locked up, buried alive or dead, I observed the world through a crack in the tower wall, it was always narrow, cylindrical rooms with a view on the world I had lost.

One day I will list the prisons I've visited in reality, hence high gates, bars, wire, loaded devices engineered to trigger well-honed states of culpability. And I bear as a wound the blows from Eve, my mother's surprise imprisonments. As she tells it, my mother was never in prison. When I was in jail, she would say, locating, via antonomasia, prison in a jail to which she and her fellows had the only keys.

Let's add the relegation of this very book, held within the iron bars of a cage for an indefinite period

Vaguely on her guard, H? or me? keeps safe, sitting on the terrace of an imaginary café on the edge of an imaginary river, that flows through Osnabrück or Strasbourg, watching the dates and hypotheses go by, ghostly mannequins, shelves of still-living books, murmuring: 'If this was the last book, if it was stillborn, if it was in intensive care,'

Language, what have you to say about this world that hesitates

And the world drops death? I find you too weak and ill-equipped

Language, try harder, I'm over here, I await

Your raft

Is anything more of a book than the *Raft of the Medusa*, more tangled more hanging on tight than all the mythological passages, the frantic Pesachs jostled by the hot flashes of ordinary terror? There's a narrow rapport between shipwrecks and the books I cling to

Wednesday, April 8, panic aboard the Pesach, as I noted on page 50

However, with wind in our sails still and masses of canvas, the body flies up like a ship cast out of the sea, the horror! we spin in immense concentric circles, the room has lost its walls in space, no time left before the fall, and so as not to crash, we dive like fools into the whirlpool, the soul spins like a top, down we go, we plummet, I

In this state of terrified intoxication, falling like Icarus, I see, off the dream's left wing, the stable rectangle studded with centuries-old oaks and pines that serves as our raft, moored for the nonce in Élisée Reclus Street

Nana comments on the street name: predestined for us. Yet the street really exists, indifferent to its name.

The painting, I see perfectly well, is *Portrait of the year 2420*, after Thucydides. I am in it. On my left, land. A tiny person ploughs the earth in the old way, saws branches, prunes them, like the peasant hitched to his plough in the painting brilliantly projected onto canvas by the visionary soul of Pieter Bruegel, father, son, disciple or imitator, or if it's not the work of Bruegel, then it's by Daedalus

Falling, foundering like the Duke of Clarence plunged head first into the mortal wine butt of his nightmare and already long dead before he finally manages to die, we film and in a loop project the final instants of his dying day after day, this drowning in the sea lasts a long time, it seems to go on for eternities, if only we weren't simultaneously prey to a wretched dizziness, and the worst is it goes on and on this caricature of life, this long, drawn-out dying that is death's ferociousness

Ten thousand years I've been falling, Icarus thinks

Icarus is me, the author thinks, except there is no author. Pieter Bruegel had been dead for ages when a painting was painted after one of his dreams

And when the crowds, the masses, the armies of the dead surge, when the 'terrible people' crowd the pages of a Report on life's excluded people, called 'the lifeless' in the accounts composed in his language by Daniel Defoe, most brilliant descendant of Thucydides

the author, the very idea of author or painter of this or that plague or pestilence is inevitably buried under the number of victims and their allegory

take, for instance, the *Journal of the Plague Year*; of the 11,550 lines of this account, three alone are devoted, in a marginal note towards the end, to the author, wherein latecomers to his tale will discover this minor figure's fate, one four-thousandth of the total dead over a few cruel months. Moreover, we must note, this Servant of Memory who has responded with zeal, humility and compassion to his mission, and with the moral rigour of a Kafka faithful to his post as an Insurance Agent, only occupies this fraction of a page as someone interred in the fourth of five new cemeteries created in great haste to deal with the extraordinary violence and rapidity of London's Great Plague

'The author of this journal lies buried in that very ground, being at his own desire, his sister having been buried there a few years before,' says the unsigned note respectful of the anonymity of the reporter, who may or may not be the author,

we fall, Icarus is us, we have been falling for ten thousand years

and no one to say who will paint this *Fall of Icarus*, we know only the dates. The Fall began at noon in May 1594; shortly before he expired Mercator left the map of the world that allows us to locate ourselves in the absence of landmarks; we didn't fall any old way, that is what produces the strange non-Euclidian beauty of my fateful voyage, says Icarus, we were piloting the representation of the world to come,

in conformity with the profound truth of great epistemological events, we may say the painting is not by its author, its originality lies in Mercator's stroke of brilliance,

as soon as this great mathematician-geographer had his Vision of the world as if seen from the sun although he was home in Holland, his vision spread like wildfire across the entire country, do you see the idea's splendour? Yesterday at noon we the human species lived as in the year 79 of Pliny the Elder whose every light was extinguished in five minutes by the volcano's eruption, the next day at noon we live 2,000 years from yesterday; stretched on the grass of a spring meadow we watch the acrobatics of machines, seagulls and airplanes, all mixed together, the astronautic super-planes evolving freely two thousand metres over the cats' heads and mine

We see perfectly that some figures, on earth on the left side of the painting, live in one century, faces bowed to the earth, the earth is free of cadavers, while on the right side of the painting, others are simultaneously dying in another century where airplanes do nose dives and the sea is stuffed with human and non-human wrecks

When I was a Poilu, Icarus says, I died by the millions, I remember 22 August 1914, on that day 17,000 copies of me died at once, the night before I'd written a letter to my mother, it said: I am doing fine, I am in one piece, send me some of those little Easter cakes

We know, I tell my daughter

Those who are about to fall into the barrel of nothingness always write a long or short letter, whatever the author's insignificance, what is strongest of all is the course of the stream

I owe a life to the Supernational Nation of the Sacrificed. According to the generals, whose brains are puffed up with stripes and medals, the Sacrificed, ordained Soldiers without

Solidus, are destined to be killed on the spot by their hundreds of thousands. What counts is that the killable be replaceable by an equal number of killable. What matters to me is that they write.

Writers one and all, by the hundreds of thousands, poets and millions of poems, millions of psalms to mop up the tears

When the foot soldier Michael Klein, later my grandfather, was killed as predicted by the Poilu model, first one or other leg ripped off on 27 July 1916 and dead before August, the bottle didn't arrive. Often when I go walking in the forest I look towards the undergrowth, maybe my grandfather's manuscript washed up here, exhausted by its cruel destinerrancy, knowing that it departed from a forest of beech and ash trees to the east of Baranovici a hundred years ago with no map of the world and the centuries to guide it

perhaps there was no soldier's poem, no letter for the unimagined times, nothing left? nothing sent? perhaps the poem, an orphan gone astray, abandoned, has lost hope in some forest, a little of grandpapa's pâté mixed with the Bielorussian earth, and I don't even know where Baranovici is

this is what happens to a foot soldier vanished without a word or funeral rites, replaced by an iron cross, such mutism demands an explanation, I ought to have asked his wife his fiancée his widow, I awoke too late, me too I buried a mute infantryman; when Elpenor the lesser, the without-any-marks-of-distinction, finds himself alone and dead who knows where, or else half drunk, an infinitesimal quantity—three feet at the

most among the epic's hundreds of thousands of phonemes—
guided by the innocence of the almostnothings, holding back
his sobs with difficulty, he summons the boss of all the battalions,
and says: I Elpenor Almost-Nothing-At-All, having been, I
wish to continue being, I have no bottle I don't know how to
write but I have my name worth its weight in gold like that of
any human calf. And Ulysses in person and divine added the
last of the foot soldiers to his multitudinous inventory of tombs,
we find it for all eternity in *The Odyssey* Canto X. What purpose
will he have served? The compassionate honour of literature

Thanks to Elpenor no one can forget that Literature is the
country with no border where no soldier remains unknown.

What's in a name, I think, again, what fate, what tale, what
philosophy? Take the name of my grandfather, in him you have
a gesture destined to fail: everyone or nearly is named Klein, at
any moment, on any genealogical chart, there's always a Klein
and almost always a Michael, our Klein is one of thousands, the
whole of Europe and later the Americas have recorded the
ephemeral, insignificant presence, the resistance of this inextin-
guishable syllable, without us, without our memories, we the
keepers and the forgetters, our Klein would be less than an
atom in the dust of the world, sometimes we think that it was
in order to fight against this lack of distinction that our grandfather had his Bright Idea: enlist in 1914 at the age of 33 in the
German army in spite of all his reasons not to: as a father of
two little daughters, aged one and three, as a faithful spouse,
doubly faithful, on the one hand to a wife, on the other to an

imperial power embodied in an Emperor archetypically poor in human love to whom our Klein owes nothing, in whom he doesn't believe, bewitched by an idea dating to the end of the nineteenth century that impels him to get killed at the Front as a Frontline soldier in order to prove that a Jew is as clayey a foot soldier as any other, a bottle filled with as much blood as any other bottle of blood, an entity subject to fate, prepared to trek across the *one thousand six hundred and forty kilometres* from Strasbourg to Baranovici in order to fall very far from his point of departure

a Jewish Icarus

For the cats Sunday, 12 April, was Liberation Day. We hadn't slept a wink. Another exodus! How frightening to imagine yourself in front of the iron door, knowing today is the day of the Passage from Inside to Outside, from Now to the thus-far-inexistent Next Time, from the familiar to the unknown, Innocence to Experience, and the winged emissary hasn't returned which, astro-physically, is a terrifying mystery, will it ever return, will it return later, it won't return, in front of the Door-Shield the Cats prepare themselves for   , already morning is still night, the sun is rising in the West, the Hour has come, one last contraction and the two Cats are cast out into the Big Wide World, we spring from finite to infinite, us Creation's First Cats, brand new little souls at the foot of the very tall old trees, the chirruping peoples, the chaotic under-growth, night's powerful fragrances

in night's quivering thickness, still sheltered from our indecision, we'd changed our minds there was zero light, the House
had asked: 'why leave the limited but risk-free comfort of Egypt
and its cuisine—out of fidelity to Nature, but what does Nature
promise?—to taunt Chance, a huge, ill-defined toy, from the
pleasure of toying with Fate, because you want to answer the
cats' naive urges, motivated as they are by a feverish desire, recognizing the timeless force of the call for "liberty" that rouses
the Living in their millions, boiling desire, that volcanic energy
whose incomprehensible power one can only salute—this voca-
tion of birth this urgency to be born and reborn

'whereas not-open the Door that has never, in the life and
memory of the Cats been opened was an abstention both effi-
cacious and non-violent, we would not open, thus guaranteeing
ourselves the peace of habit; freedom's illusion would be trans-
formed in the calm repeated suspension of the non-event, we
would not upset paradise's applecart, we would avoid blindly
plunging into storms encumbered by the hummocks and pitfalls
of life abroad, no drunken embarking on this or that extravagant
boat, we'd pass our years and our days like our fellow apartment
cats in a cosy sitting room, furnished with small precipices, end
our cushiony days like the Cave Peoples who'd never have stood
to be deprived of that which they would never have known
they might have discovered.'

in the morning, advancing across the bristling ice cubes of
the big hummocks, the ship passed no fewer than five hundred

icebergs, some of them colossal, I can't even imagine it, everywhere words and images crash, all that sticks out of these dark
masses is the word 'free', free water, free, free, free, in the staircase
the *Endurance* passes with supple undulations of its cat spine
like a person answering the call of ancestral selves, go, let's go,
letsgo!

Someone knocked at the house door three times, an irruption
of the gods, as oneiric it strikes me as the same scene in
Wuthering Heights, and at the fourth knock the Door of the
House blows open, it's over it is starting, suddenly the sharp,
perfumed forest air whiffs in nostrils and ears, and the cats
sitting stock still in the embrasure of the universe receive the
sumptuous embrace of the Theatre of Infinite Life. Time stopped

Next H spent hour after hour in the continental brushland
crisscrossed by the methodical explorers: witness, guardian,
mother duck, adorer of little goddesses descended to this stranger
on earth,

the landmass that now stretched before us was marvellously
unknown

at six in the evening my mother's voice woke me she called
Where are you? H said: I'm waiting for the explorers to return.
You are a slave to those cats, my mother said. Right afterwards
the adventurers came home: the House had become a port for

the cats. No one was wounded, lost, killed, nothing has blown up, survival has begun.

As her Bible of Auguries, H opened the great tome of the notebooks of Kafka, my grandmother Omi's contemporary, to consult its magic formulas. It was Thursday, 26 October 1910, my mother had just been born, Franz, my grandmother Omi says, writes me that possible happiness always turns impossible. Omi doesn't agree, according to her it is our primitive cowardice that makes us lead an ersatz life. Saying which, voluptuously, she pops a dark-chocolate praline into her mouth.

Is it these opposing views that decided us? I don't know, but when I threw open the Door onto majestic, thrilling and disquieting Real Life, I plunged into space with the cats beside me, without any guarantee. Michael Klein opens the Door of the beautiful house into which he has just moved, his helmet on his head, a sprig of lilac in his buttonhole, he has disguised himself with German thoroughness, he was unaware of any anxieties, looking at his two tiny daughters he doesn't think next time a boy, he thinks next time for safety's sake add a visor to the helmet, safety from what? He thought I'm enlisting doubly, as a volunteer, for Austria Hungary that I have only let go to seize with a confident leap the German trapeze, for the other Kaiser, and above all for ——————

he thought nothing the Door opened and he leapt into Nothing at All from which no acrobat returns

Fling yourself and your most precious, most pure beings into Life's Void and land unscathed on a moss-and-pine-needle-upholstered floor, imparts to the bodysoul duo a keen sense of jubilation for which you acquire a taste when you have just died, and then no, you are still alive

All these sudden departures can become a transgenerational tradition: this *Aufbruch* towards the Weg-von-Hier, the Far-from-Here, the Far that keeps a rapport with the Here, these hasty leaps into emptied time, the first time was in 1929, on that occasion Eve, later my mother, took a suitcase with which and in which she went straight to London from Osnabrück next she jumped on the occasion, as if she'd saddled up posthaste, if you can call the occasion a departure so rapid you overtake yourself, jumping onto the first train or boat or plane and the suitcase will or won't follow, the essential is to head for the Weg-von-Hier

And here we go again a hundred years later, this was in 29, the delirious year, the sick man of the century, hurry, hurry, off one rushed like wild horses, for Eve my mother being prepared was natural, the Renault 5 brand new and speedy that in reality has died of age and rust—rhymes with lost, my mother says—already on the road, once more I sped off without having observed the baggage ceremony, follow me I pray to the suitcases, at the last minute, so short so sharp, my only belongings my tartan woollen bathrobe, a true house, a camp cot, a cradle for the cats, a mother's skin in which to wrap my tired body, a boat in case of need, a small hoard of signifiers, a game of syllables and allusions, my mother already at the wheel, already moving, like a tardy angel, folded in two, I threw myself as best I could onto a seat I spread the house made of wool across our knees for the long voyage—a crazy idea, my mother says, the car had a heater, delete that bit, and already far down the road, super-speed, seeing nothing and meanwhile the Renault 5, proud even boastful, veers left zigzags nicks the cliffs, sidewinds, like a torero, feints, I was terrified, my mother impassive, like a last abode I wrapped myself in the woollen bathrobe

We are disoriented, except my mother

The world in nutshells, jetsam bobbing on a tossing and turning mental ocean

Only the dogs cats and Eve don't founder

The disaster, I say, is more than biblical, direction no longer exists neither north nor west nothing nothing exeasts

Save for my mother who goes straight ahead

Meanwhile the cats play with the world, spinning it with a divine paw-bat

I don't know myself, I don't understand myself, I surprise myself I'm jolted hither thither by fierce gusts of wind, I am dismasted

Like the rest of the world

I hide under my mother's bathrobe

I'm full of admiration for the crew of the *Endurance*, hang on, hang on, in the end we eat the dogs

Go, go, Eve says, whipping her mount, the Renault 5 gallops on

I turn in tight circles here and there, I say. We laugh

I'm looking for a place I hope exists, Champlain says, here is this way, the Spanish sailors say, we're racing towards the unknown,

I seek a place that exists, The Place latitude zero longitude zero. I'm after a point, the still point of everyplace, I seek Place, Shackleton says

Rhymes with Grace, my mother, at the helm of the Renault 5, says

I've slipped under the tartan canvas, we're not the ones moving, the icebergs shift, cliffs appear, the world moves faster than Shackleton,

The earth is bearing me away, the great difficulty for our navigation is that place itself flees us, all that counts is momentum being dead is not a problem my mother says, I'm going Weg-von-Hier

We're trying to advance, Shackleton says, the dream is to Advance but we see that the world is what moves, space twists, solidity crevasses, we rush towards the Immobile,

Everything bears us away and everything repels us, the ground quakes under the nutshells of our hulls,

from number to number, from date to date, lean in and fight the world that blows and blows and separates us from the Paradise of Immobility

Only numbers are stable, place escapes us, Shackleton says, save in dream, save aboard the R5 *Endurance*. We career helter-skelter towards the spot where dawn and dusk last for six months each, where dawn dusks dawn and winter is summer where the sun sets rising,

Place escapes us, what remains is the account, what remains is the tale

On 20 April everything was close to black, between the outside walls of the dream, the Stage: a simple strip of bare cement. There was no sun. I felt nostalgic for light and therefore shadows. The beloved's Shadow was in the shade. A Shade without shadow, and pained to be dead. I worried about the dead, they are so fragile, except my mother.

If the Earth was just a poisoned hazelnut you might well doubt the point of being alive, I was thinking

Meanwhile the cats are playing in the world. They return to recount their adventures:

Prodigious, unknown forces are at work in the terrestrial zone. Today it rained. First the rain stretched its damp grey cloth over the world and drenched the trees in a dense absence of colour. Next the rain increased its thicknesses, its depth. For three hours the cats sat on the windowsill at the edge of the rain. At noon, Isha took the plunge. She ran across the garden, further and further, ridges and hedges rose up, earth's surfaces diminished, till they came to the known world's far edge. Then, in no hurry, she returned, soaked, and calmly settled at the edge of the rain wrapped in her beautiful, rain-coloured fur. Willy-nilly, Haya was right behind her. Today was Rain. They have learnt about rain.

I am the cats

I was living vicariously

I've a cat in my breast

Before dawn on Thursday, 23 April, Haya's urgent, impatient call rang out: The Door! The Door! The Door!

Afraid that Haya will wake the dead, H suffers cedes. The Door opens. The Haya arrow, metaphor incarnate, spurts a motionless silver line, 90 kilometres an hour like a reproach. Quick! Quick! Life! Me, Life! They are waiting for me, I am waiting for myself, off I go, no time wasted. By whom? By the infinite. Don't you see the infinite in the kingdom of Liberty, the promise, its humid moiré night tulle, its over-thereness over-there? That's where I'm going, me the flesh around the word liberty, the handful of letters to name the nameless, I am the answer, an answer that sparkles, a three-kilogram goddess painted in silver and ermine and ebony lacquer, I am the dazzling demonstration, I am the speed of life itself, the flickering yes

The cats lead / I direct them / The cats come / I am the mouse

Albertinage

The Tale intends to play on Albertine's Life and Love as long as the sources and resources of desire continue to track her deathsresurrections, each chapter is staged in a different room in the house, each room being an occasion to put into play, as in one of the fateful establishments where Dostoyevski plays at Russian roulette, a dramatic action, a head-whirling wager on death or flight. In the preamble, for which we are not present, it is probable that the Subject H or I as cat, has managed to kidnap Albertine from the lush and remote landscapes of the garden, and taking her in her teeth, neither wounding nor giving her a chance to flee, a trickle of saliva dribbling from her mouth, has set her free in the prison of the House. Cut to the ardent protagonists of this passion in the living room, furiously engaged in this anxious love, both of them in the grips of incertitude, to flee or not to flee, delighting in their terrors and painful hopes, in a frenzy of desire that alone allows us to feel existence's beauty and need. On the Cat's face, features tense with devotion's trance, you can read the grave expression, the religious mystery of the folly of the love for which one would die or even kill, from vital, irresistible allegiance to the demands of our nature. This is fulfilment's violent hour.

Workmanlike, the cats busy themselves around the folds of a big parasol lying on the floorboards that represents a beached sailing ship. Going and coming, searching the great overturned vessel, neither alive nor dead, switched off. In this world with all its intestinal folds, Albertine has taken refuge. Perfectly inaudible, invisible, frozen in the immobility of the besieged, holding her breath—but not her smell. She has been scented. You cannot stop being a mouse.

I saw the cats' effervescence. Didn't perceive Albertine's scent. I read the scene and I interpreted. I followed the doings of the cats. Twists in the Tale's plot took us from room to room, from living room to my mother's bedroom, from Eve's bedroom to Nana's room. I never saw Albertine, I saw her virtually via the cats' sudden shifts of direction. She was a lively small creature some five centimetres long, excellent instincts, an exceptional creature who was obviously testing the mettle of the cats. It was a tragedy. It occurred to me she might win on points. After all, between Albertine and the narrator who wins our hearts? I admired her. I admitted that I loved her, that she was beautiful, that there was nothing I could do, the audience is powerless.

Love's charm is desire condemned to frustration, the promise of loss at the very heart of possession, refusal embedded in refuge.

Towards evening, I gathered up the body. It was lukewarm. It weighed no more than a sheet of paper, the weight of the lost life. In my view she wasn't dead. She had gone to her death like Cleopatra. In the prime of life. Or like Albertine astride her own destiny. I buried her on 24 April.

Between April 21 and May 1, we conveyed ourselves into the Log of the Ship *Endurance*. Compared with the K Notebook, *Endurance* was a tub.

I don't know why I keep travelling between two notebooks, with some pocket versions on the side. Perhaps because the expedition is always more than a single vessel. The captain is naturally haunted by the idea that one of the two might sink. During the voyage one ship plays dead. The captain, however, doesn't know which one

We don't know where we're going, from ship to another ship, from this dream to that, from one century into the next, hopeful and at large. We hope to return to ourselves in fifty or more likely a hundred years, if we are still alive.

Which is why I imagine nothing at all. Beyond the hedge I will not be, hence I'm not there, hence I'm not.

It's not impossible to exist without time. This can happen. It's like in the City: having been gutted then embalmed in a reality as strange still as a Continent-surprise, the City has never been more visible, considerably more affirmative than it was when its population acted as a screen. It is in these virgin circumstances, without parallel, totally foreign

I don't recall a first of May this sombre, stormy, rain-rain-rainy, lights out, as dictated by the Obscure Circumstances—the powerful Unknown Conditions designated in the papers by the acronym OC or UC—in case some lightweight among the human populace believed, by some outmoded memory, that today is the day for nosegays and fiesta. When you wake in the perpetual darkness in Antarctica it may be that for a second, as when you strike a match in a labyrinth with neither east nor west, you picture yourself opening your eyes in your room on the Old Continent and immediately reality turns black. You don't get accustomed to it. Waking up in total Blackness still makes most of us panic. Except for the cats. You feel your way, you cry out. Everything is Black, you are frightened, you don't understand. A brother on the telephone, shouting:

My sister, what's going on? Everything is black? It's daybreak and it doesn't break. I got up. I showered. All black. I ate my breakfast. Still nothing. This total night. How is this happening? I am stupefied!

Give me back my identity card, I say to the guard, a big guy, who I thought looked nice enough when he demanded *my papers*. A guy who looked at me derisively, flapped his large, closed hand in my face, then opened it and mockingly offered me two small gold-coloured effigies. I had a horrible presentiment. My Identity Card, I repeated, louder. Without my *Carte d'Identité*. I couldn't leave the country. The man played dumb. Then he told me to follow him. I imagined the worst—I acted as if nothing was amiss, while trying to think of a way out of this situation. Alas. We took a few steps in the street, he glanced at my legs and said: but they're not thin, are they? I should have worn trousers I said. For I was wearing shorts. The City had been flushed out like a barrel. We walked along the Rue des Écoles. They're dismantling the Sorbonne I told myself. The building lay on its side, a gutted carapace, a fossil. Nothing remained of a long, far-off history but a pack of yellowing images, no memories even, scraps of withered dreams. A deserted carcass, not even a whale skeleton, and the word *dismantle*. I didn't even remember Rabelais. Just the word. I examined it curiously, I dressed and undressed it, it writhed like some deranged thing, I felt stark raving mad too. I was nothing, less than nothing. This all seemed devoid of sense. In the middle of the street someone whose name I've forgotten brought me a little knitted cap, of greyish linen, unwearable, it's too small, I said, giving it back, it looked like an abandoned bird nest. The cap turned inside out, into a jester's cap with a green point and a wide tongue of bright red dangling over the face down to the chin. A fool's cap! I would definitely not go unnoticed in the grey streets. But by whom? The once-crowded boulevards were clean entrails. I wore the cap for nobody. Just when the cop was going to drag me into his den, his secretary appeared, she was leaving, I grabbed her by the arm and cried: come with us, this gentleman is going to give me back my Identity Card. Surprised, she followed me, so I had a witness. The only real person in all this nightmare. Him furious, tricked. The man returned my precious document with a hellish grimace. Saved! And Hades vanished.—Don't you know that you should never let go of your Identity Card? At your age, Reason told me. If he'd known

I was eighty-three years old, I thought. But when I am dressed hidden under my paper make-up, no one suspects.

Never let go of your official papers.

In the brouhaha of Wind, 1 May, I tell my daughter—we were swimming, the water on her side calm, the air, enraged—I have lots of small worries that come together and make one big worry. When she asks me what the little worries are, I no longer remember, they scatter to every corner of my body. Finally, I say: Everything is conditional. How do you write that? my daughter says. I'll have to ask the paper, I say. As I well knew. When you are in over your head the important thing is to write it down. Immediately I worried about the translation. Change the colour of the language and everything sinks like a stone. Whole pages drown

Tuesday, 5 May: when I reread the previous page, I thought at first that it was from long ago, that it dated from some middle-aged period intoxicated with worries and anxieties, like that total obsessive described in the *Journal of the Plague Year*, back then I was unhinged, everywhere people were dying and dead; panicked, cowering inside myself, if I could have plugged all my ears, the ears of my thoughts and afterthoughts, I was thinking and listening to myself thinking: end up in this way, locked down, life a blank, what a dreadful fate, not a smile, zero memory and impotence limited only by a notebook page, luckily there is paper, the encouraging whiteness, as effective as a face mask, and a notebook, I still arm myself with them. (All these shivers of thought in French.) Fortunately, there's language, its urge to laugh, its hoard of words

Moreover, even when I don't think I have a single sentence or reflection left to write, even when my mouth is full of insipid stones, it turns out that all I have to do is point the pen at the blank sheet and the two promptly pair up, wed, express themselves, esteem each other and the pen has only to pursue the invisible traces that light up at its approach along the notebook's pathways.

I owe my life to our ancestor the goose feather

To return to the previous page, which made me think of an old abyss repelling my shaky speleology, it turned out that she alit there on 1 May, a short calendar-time ago. But the time malady that we all suffer from means that sometimes we are pushed into uncontrollable haste, we race on ahead of ourselves, time careers past us, a whole night in three minutes, while at other times time stands still, in vain we wait for it, it doesn't come, it doesn't come, the old rhythms, worn out, are paralyzed. This handful of calendar days have gone on for so long that they seem to have taken place a year ago

And now look: this morning, the today of a year ago reminds me of the sleeper who wakes up thinking he's in his old bedroom, a brand new and keen disquiet, not at all phantasmic, my very own, wounds me, nourished by so many choked-off sobs that made my chest swell, right here, in this study, in the year 2018 which comes back now, as if for the first time, again I weep again for Philia and Aletheia alternatively or both at once, with the very tears that I first spilt when my beloved was snatched away and everything started over, the same old pain, now too heavy now too feeble, recommences now is yesterday again

Why are you crying? Isha appears in front of me, stares into the depths of my pupils, holds my gaze in her own supernatural immensity and thinks. Thinks, thinks, thinks, thinks deeper, thinks harder: want want want. Look: I am Philia, reborn. Holds out her soul, prepares to fire off a word. To talk is like melodious sighing, you open your mouth and ah! from the bottom of your heart out darts a coloured arrow. Isha wants to be a talking species, her entire being tenses, her soul pants, with all my being, lungs tensed soul arched I accompany her, I wait, ears pricked mine and hers mine she me, and all of a sudden

I myself am transported by the most violent curiosity. Oh! What will be her first word, don't let her stop, my thoughts were whirling, I was like an astrophysicist who refuses to die before having seen the centuries-long-awaited illumination, I didn't take my eyes off hers as if I could guide her thinking across the abyss to speech, as if I did what Dante did but *in reality*. Clearly there was no more time, only the extreme tension of our two conjoined wills and suddenly—you will think I'm hallucinating—but what I say is truer than true, it's the Truth, and were that not the case the paper that breathes under the pen would revolt, grow cold as marble, I couldn't write a word—

listen, suddenly, clearly, like a clarion call of her small voice so recognizable for its limpidity and its resonance, suddenly she spat out two sounds, two gold bubbles, two perfectly formed, real words, two clear notes, her large eyes joining mine, her whole body vibrant as a musical instrument, and I saw her collect her strength, I sensed her all-powerful desire to speak even if it cost her life

you won't believe it, I tell my daughter, Isha spoke. She said two words

Two words? My daughter looks cautious, prudent, sceptical. I hesitated to say something so majestic, so impressive in a case so extraordinary and probably one of its kind. I hesitated to confide my secret. I approached it by circling this small, earth-shattering meteor. Something like 'Je suis / *I am*' I say, afraid of my daughter's scepticism or disappointed expression.

What language was she speaking? my daughter asks.

French, I say. This was true. This was good.

Do you think it's a hallucination? I ask

Yes. But a lovely one. Addressing cats, one never uses the first person. One employs verbs in the second person.

The armchair squeaked. I dared to think: the armchair is speaking. Speaking wicker

I wished to pull my daughter into our sphere of the marvellous, vainly would I have tried to hypnotize her, neither her eyes nor mine are supernatural enough

Perhaps she said, '*Viens* / Come'? my daughter suggested.

Good idea! *Come* has no *I*.

Yes, yes, I say. My daughter said: Yes. Carried away by my stupefaction, I repeated: Yes? As if to verify that my hearing wasn't playing tricks on me. Then she said: Yes. Yes. Distinctly. And in French, I say, thrilled, and relieved to have, despite my fears, managed to speak the modest truth. She said: *Oui*. She didn't say: *Yes*. What bliss to be able to say the whole truth.

That I can believe, my daughter says. Her meowing's phonology is French.

Who cares if they call such an event a hallucination. What's important is that it really happened.

Here are the facts: Isha and I were in the kitchen. She stood up—she can walk on her hind legs, which are slender and elegant—standing tall in front of the glass door, she reached for the handle, a little too high, turned to me and her whole body's attitude said: Open! Open! So I said: You want to go out? I had understood the signs perfectly, this, however, was when she took the leap into the other language. If I think about it, this simple private scene was in truth more than what actually happened.

Everything was more, and happened not only in the kitchen but also in a consecrated space. The door is also the Door to the neighbouring world and while difficult of access, the cover of a book that waits to be read in order to cease being a rock. Open is the key (the word) to all the realms of knowledge.

According to Isha, what matters most in her exchanges with us and especially with me, is speed: the message must pass quickly, quickly. It's urgent. Natural rhythms determine this urgency: life is shorter than life, Isha is twice as fast as me, our exchanges require on the one hand patience, on the other impatience. Which is why she likes winged messages, monosyllables, sighs and all the lightning-fast vocables, open, fast, go, come, no, god, jump, want, yes,

On Saturday, 29 February of the last year, we were fine. No one imagined that this day dusted in finest gold was one of the last. On we went.

Destiny filmed us from behind, we the blind unaware that on this road winding so agreeably among the tufts of broom and sea vistas, we were printing out the last footsteps of a yesteryear doomed to melt like snow

We went towards History's next chapter as children towards the next holiday, as heroes towards the next wedding, and had no idea that under the word 'holiday' lurked the unknown. I was counting on continuing from this last day in February to my mission's end, going on from stage to stage, ensuring that I bore my dead in good condition to the quay. A marvellous gold fog appeared at dawn, draping the pines in strange bridal veils

Under such conditions, Shackleton says, our usual perspectives are all skewed, the world is strangely animated, pack-ice undulates, mists flit between rock and rock, concealing them, landmarks flee, great mountainous peaks all of a sudden loom up, icebergs advance like Carnival-on-Ice floats, and the *Endurance* is pinned who-knows-where for all of the inflexible eternity that rises between winter and spring. I add that seals are much rarer than squirrels in the forest. Beyond doubt we lose sight of earth and even the illusion of a lost paradise.

And having become, irrefutably, a ghost, I had, instead of a sense of ordinary reality, the feeling that all the people who yesterday were familiar have been ghosted overnight, the night of 29 February to 1 March. How my friends felt I didn't know, I didn't dare tell them what was happening: all of us had been severed from reality, friendship's telephone number and even the habits that support our daily navigation.

Yesterday was already the olden days, it is undeniably a strangely long time ago that we were making plans with numerous digressions, foreseeing stops along the Road, taking our time, like Jacques and his Master, consuming quantities of time's renewable liquidity, we had the 'schedule' thing under control, as well trained as our sled dogs, which keep the secret of exact distance in all their muscles, Shackleton thought, in the brain's control room we had a map of planet Earth and of talking continents with which we programmed dates and hoped-for meeting places in the year to come, we moved from one camp to the next, in every case, we used the word 'next' or 'soon', those exhilarating superlatives

Yesterday-once-upon-a-time I thought it could happen, for example in the 1940s, those years of mythic dislocation, that we might go so far as to believe, without too much effort, that we did not fully believe, we pitched our tent in the shadows and in thunder but we kept in reserve some of the belief dust, enough for us to reckon on the hypothesis of a future, with a bit of luck, we would surely arrive safe and sound, and failing that, the world would march on without us

One day the end would end, the ice would loosen its grip, sieges are not eternal, the condition of shipwreck would thaw, overnight forever and no longer would end their desperate embrace, prison walls would relent, we could even say 'one day' without the locution's vagueness having an effect of annulation, of the extinction of the distant, promising gleam

30 April 2420

In order not to lose all trace of these mutilated pasts abruptly deprived of their chance at memory and which no anniversary will now recall to the present, and since the old moments of life sink with deadly speed towards the point of no-return, in the space of three minutes a day goes by, the ship spins ever deeper into the moonless well, and in truth, is already swallowed up, I gather a few dates fallen from the tree, still green like acorns but promised in no time to desiccations and dispersal, for the most part already eviscerated, last passwords for events once grand and venerable as the empires of philosophers peoples plagues civilizations that in a single day recorded twenty thousand dead, twenty thousand learned volumes and twenty thousand monuments, and have disappeared as totally as if they had never been,

I dreamed. Thanks to the dream I dictated a brilliant book at fantastic speed to the Man Friday seated at my side—this book went by so quickly I wouldn't have had time to write or read it, it was torrential but, nonetheless, composed of sparkling and well-tempered sentences, crystals, gemstones, I scarcely perceived their writing, fortunately my man secured these treasures whose value I was unaware of but could sense, one time I saw the word 'grenade' ping I would have liked to take it, turn it over, examine it, Grenade, which Grenade? Granada the Arab, the pomegranate's fruit, the weapon? I didn't even have time to mull over my curiosity, in one corner of my dream the expert in precious stones assembled an entire chasuble from these sonorous gems. An instant, not even a second, a lightning flash, I could Imagine these cabochons were dates, sorts of diamond-headed pins stuck in the gauze of a time-memory quick to dissolve, each of them fixing the substance and circumstances of all sorts of very rich hours in our histories. Reporting the dream's state of mind, I realized I had been present unawares at this mysterious operation called sublimation. Did I regret not knowing the book? No. I was filled with satisfaction without a shadow of melancholy. All is metamorphosis. All is different

I myself don't remember what I've written. There was a flame. Then ashes surely, then nothing. A pinch of. Something alive was deposited on the sheets

It is good to write under the influence of Forgetting, I tell myself. A humid and fragrant humus covers all that is picked up, carried away, rolled under the divine scrolls of Oblivion, declared dead, whereas there is no death that hasn't the power to resuscitate

I write with a gold cabochon cut in the image of a goose quill. Ages ago I forgot the goose. I forgot the goose. However, I can feel my fingers quiver when a sentence takes off. I don't know how many geese were mobilized to write Baudelaire's poems. What I owe to the billions of geese that lived so that I may turn up, too late, on the raft of the notebook

I owe one piece of luck to the pines that die to transport us to Lethe's other quay

I've forgotten everything

Without the dates deposited here and there along the Path where the eternal Charon sings, absolutely nothing would remain of the long long long year whose desert we have just crossed with the rapid sluggishness of a sleeper between one departure and another arrival on earth.

There was, they say, month-minutes. These are the months that pass in their entirety at great terrestrial speed. The opposite of torture-days that go on for interminable month-halts

From the first night after the last night before Saturday, 2 October 2002, I have forgotten everything, then

From Wednesday, 12 February 2020, all is erased

Remains

According to historians the flow began to coagulate on 12 February

According to me that was a Wednesday

According to me the day that my father turned into a kepi was a Saturday. He popped his head around the front door and it was someone else. So I too was someone else. My father was outside in disguise, a stranger's head

According to my son Oblivion and Noblivion are but a single twin. You noblivion in order not to oblivion. There is something surreptitiously sweet about forgetting. You doublivion to remind yourself of the world's other side. Doubling Oblivion permits you to pass from the singular to the universal. At times I am dazzled by the violence of Forgetting, at times by the sublime violence of the birth of Oblivion. Forgetting, you are a thief. Forgetting, you right wrongs

Oblivion, it seems, trumps Love. Some say Love trumps Oblivion. Me, I seesaw. I note that when I write I forget everything. Absolutely everything. Except the Rest. Maybe what is written is the Rest. I want to write the cries. My hand won't go fast enough, unlike in the old days my hand is not winged.

Once All's forgotten the unforgettable remains

Oblivion, my son says, whereupon I'm dazzled by so much illumination I forget what Oblivion is

We clamber up the greening side of an amiable mountain like a friendly and helpful donkey on whose back hospitable spirits have, at intervals, planted little wooden signposts with human indications: *goat path*, *this way to the reed beds*, we are already at 937 metres, I think I see an allusion to the year of my birth, this is when I feel, not without emotion, that I'm forgetting the earth. This is not a dream. Up we climb.

'Weclimb!' It's how I cheer on my cats, when we set off past the species border.

There is a well-mowed meadow, in the centre a bright yellow flower: the word *Antan / Yesteryear / Of old.* What bliss to find it again! A real buttercup. One of humanity's treasures. Almost everyone in the land of the French language is mysteriously moved by the melody of the syllables *bouton d'or.* What is its secret charm, I wonder. It is a word you feel everyone cherishes, discretely, for its very ancient and forever young powers, just like the sound, for any Respirant, of 'mama'.

If I say *Antan,* I say to my daughter, what do you hear?

My daughter contemplates her cup of tea, I hum *Antan, Antan,* it strikes me

that these golden notes are perhaps nothing more than the title of the book in which we have been living for the last little while, which has been carrying us up hill and down dale. My daughter says the word several times, tastes it: it is a rosy and fragrant tea, it has the savour of surreality that emanates from all of India, I hear *Antan, hantan, en temps,* she dreams, as if the word cast a powerful spell. I hear and think nothing, she says, difficult to think something about a word without its context.

Don't you see how yellow and lacquered and dazzling among all vocables it is? I ask.

Do you feel that ancient need for happiness that blows through in our lungs and that is in itself a strange consolation?

If I say '*d'antan*' / *of yesteryear*?

—Ah! *D'antan*! Of yesteryear! Of old! my daughter, delighted, says, like someone who might be one of the mouse folk among whom we recognize Kafka's long, vacillating silhouette. Now there's a syntagm whose delicacy and nostalgia makes it priceless. As if the temporality out of which its name is carved affected the nature of the objects it modifies.

All these objects made of a saved past, enhanced by the past, all these moments and fragments saved, brought back from death and decay by the mysterious force of being properly named. All these disappearances changed into fonctors of oblivion. Even if very distant, they still work.

And there you have it: *d'antan* / *of old* still goes off and comes back, even if Villon, its father is lost, no feeling person on this earth will have been able to live without his syntagm's aura. Its star continues to shine and shines on this need, this *Verlangen* which stands in for time's breath in this horrible year 2420 after the (Greek) poet of old

VI
KAFKA AT THE POOL

Zu müde

I don't write. I haven't the time. In the desert there isn't any. It has all dried up. We are all strangely desiccated, seen head-on we are surprisingly pale as if all the colour had drained from us, from behind, we are flat, diminished in thickness, almost no buttocks. Weak sensations of embarrassment traverse us, the idea that it's just this way, in this kind of flimsy envelope, that apprentice ghosts with indecisive silhouettes come to visit us.

Nothing kept Kafka from his writing, especially not the most dire of catastrophes. This was the day millions died, 31 July 1914. The 31st *es ist allgemeine Mobilisierung*, the mobilization of everyone on pain of death, whence the mobilization of one recluse for his writing. A single battle, write for dear life, Kafka says. Self-preservation. *Es ist mein Kampf um die Selbsterhaltung.*

As for me, many catastrophes cut off my tongue at the root. At the very moment when I most need its help, it goes missing, no longer stirs, nailed between my teeth. And not only my tongue. My lungs, inert, not a wisp of breath. Instead of breathing's familiar in and out, the breath blocked within stony lobes, a rocky ridge whose sharp edges occupy the whole of my chest—
————I await the end

No point in any call. No response. Pain itself is mute. Anguish strangles it.

Now it was 2 August. All by himself K, the ultimate Recluse, is an army. This morning Germany declared war on Russia. Everything is crystal clear. *Let's go to the swimming pool.* Between the war and the pool, it's war. The Recluse at the pool. Alone in the water against the Artillery on parade. Flowers, hurrahs, cheers. Splash. Schwimmschule. The school of life is the Pool.

Did Michel Klein parade around shouting 'Hurrah!'? At the age of thirty-three I make quite a discovery, K says. At thirty-three, I feel some spite, some jealousy and hate for the combatants, for whom I ardently hope the worst. And I adore writing. But Michael Klein parades, face astonished, attentive, lips pursed, eyes black.

At the swimming pool, the march of time is dependably subjective.

Out in the street the infantry marches to history's beat.

Fuck the war! K thinks and dives head first into writing's pool

At the beach, in the water, we are washed of jealousy and violence

People talk to each other in the sea. There's a refuge. I could write in the water. There's no downside

Despite everything I'll write. The verb despitewrite, Kafka says

Today, 21 May 2020, having been wandering for months, I expected nothing. I tried to accept the blankness. I went so far as to counsel myself to accept my death / my end

It worked, almost

I received the Title of this book to which I had bid farewell as to my brother. I was dead: a state that is foreign to me, that deprives one of any meaning, any direction. Whoever has wandered in the desert for several weeks is familiar with this sort of starkness

You strip yourself of (space, time, worlds, world),

You lose the sea

During the desert, all the limp, blank time when you wander in the desert *you had no mirror*. You never knew how old you were, how long the day was, or lasted. Lacking a mirror, you had neither future, nor figure. That is when *Rêvoir* was composed. What one didn't believe in the light of day, one saw differently

Those you haven't seen for years you now saw, thanks to the Rêvoir technique: Since Homer nothing has changed, except the prices and the sacrifices at the Entry: you must descend underground and proceed to the ticket booth. Remember to take a warm sweater: it will be cold soon. However burning they may be, deserts ice over

To reach the Title, all of a sudden there it was, alreadythere:

Rêvoir

Everything started with Shakespeare's Sonnet 81 in which the eyes of readers not yet created posthume, eyes of pre-ghosts impatient for the future and tongues to come, as well as dreams to transport you by all available means to visitors come from time's hinterland.

Contrary to my expectations, the first Shade to alight from the Dream Elevator is not my mother, Ulysses says.

Me too, I say, stepping up to Rêvoir's Revolving Door, I was sure I'd see my mother, my roots and my sky.

But the Dream was a classic one. One of those Lover's Dreams for some We-Meet-Again Novel. The title: 'Dinner with D'.

The Dream called me on the phone:

I was invited to dine with D my philosopher friend. Imagine! He was still alive. And I hadn't seen him in such a long time, not since our last conversation, just before the end. Now nearly twenty years later I dreamt he was still alive. I was in the dream, it was still early. My sweater was too thin, later I would be cold. Besides, it was too early, after so many years I was getting carried away. Remember the charming little restaurant in the Latin Quarter, Rue Descartes? I don't wish to remember, I want to be back there. We walked down the street. And here's D walking towards us! After so many years. I was touched. Both of us are at some distance from reality. D asks: May I lean on you? Are you solid enough? Oh! How it chimed and gleamed, the word Solid. Of course, I say. And I offered him my shoulder. He puts his arm around my shoulder, tests its solidity. I'm strong, I told myself. I can do this. Not that I am that solid. All the same I'll manage. It's my soul that decides. We walked a few steps in this manner. He leans. I support him: Who'd have thought?! Do you remember? How ill you were. You even jumped out the window! And here we are. You are the sole survivor. All dead. You alone are still alive! You haven't changed. Your voice. Your hair. We spoke of delicate matters.

Later I ask: what can I call a book that doesn't know what time it is, nor the difference between night and day nor between memory and the future, whose streets end in ruins?

He says, Rêvoir: see again, see in a dream.

It was the beginning of June in October, it wasn't a week. For the soul it was a succession of snowstorms of holes in the ice of a desert place, sharp peaks crevasses of whale muzzles and plane crashes in all directions. I imagined a *Lighthouse*. A Beacon? People were laughing at it. A thick, hardened snowbank and Visible from far away, two glittering dates, painful dates: 31

May 2020, the martyrdom of George Floyd in Minneapolis, the same day as the annihilation of Joan of Arc, the smoke carried a smell of charred mares, all of Rouen was coughing, 4 June, the Tiananmen butchery, no one knows how many bodies surrendered their souls to History. Only dogs and the cats can clear paths with such ardour.

The night of 31 May (the Joan of Arc night) I spent hours eating all I could eat: I had seen K gobbling a mountain of white rice. At the sight of these mounds of white grain, an abundant manna, my hunger returns. A ghostly barking, you felt pity. I wasn't even aware of my appetite prior to that vision. Part of the night I spent with my face stuck to the dream's windowpane, trying to make the affecting food reappear. I was opposed to the idea that the Dream Reservoir was empty.

It was growing late. I was about to get up but the Dream held me back: wait a moment, you'll see! It was already almost daybreak, and I saw:

It was the very First Time. A Life together! Not only had I never imagined such a thing, not in the first life nor in the second, not hoped nor evoked, not once, nor had this ever come about in a dream. And yet I foresaw it all, lived it all from the start of the After Life. I had been visited hundreds of times, so many surprises, so many scares and jubilations, ecstasies, etc. But *That*, never. The very idea of desiring such a strange experience! Live under the same roof: never would this have crossed my mind. The principle, from the word go, was Never. The word 'roof', never. Yet not only had you returned, but also for once we were having a *Life Together*. The word Together resonated. We'd be living together from now on—my incredulity brought me up short. Not you. It was the first morning. All day I was sluggish, restrained as I was by my surprise. We'd dined together. And I was so preoccupied that I failed to think of making it a celebration, as if I had been late for a birth. Realizing this, I lost more time. In short, I was overwhelmed. Disassembled. 'We had slept.' This I registered. Now you were getting ready, soon you'd be going out. 'What on earth are you doing?' I asked myself. There I was, dithering, dazed. Logically, I should dress. What to wear? Oh! I should have planned ahead, chosen, the most elegant sweater, the most refined, dazzle him. And where is he going? Why didn't I question him, make him talk, oh listen to him, listen, gather the pearls of his wisdom, on what topics would he have enlightened me? I was in a daze, slowed down by the immensity of what had happened. I stay beside him, shadow of the Shadow, tangential. What am I doing here now, immobile? I'm waiting. From a few metres away, I watch. And—and? And what if I were thinking, revelling in it all instead of sluggish as some domestic wraith. And—And? What if I followed him? Destiny stretched my nerves to the breaking point, I was glued like a limpet to him. And—and? And if I thought, what if I enjoyed the situation instead of clinging like a limpet? There! He's opening the door. From where I am, beside myself, I adore him. Others demonstrate their savoir-faire, their aplomb. As for me? I don't even know how to turn these hours, this night, this new day into the happening it is. Come on!

Wake up! Get cracking! Time, wait for me! Let's get ready!
Make up the lost time

I am reprising the dream. It was a bit short on joy. Hard to congratulate myself. Such an occasion and pretty much wasted? I
took note of the double silence. Between him and me, not a
word? Little by little the shadow of a thought formed. Was it
that we could only Live-Together—dead? But at the very
moment this thought took shape, the Shadow slipped away,
astonished I woke.

VII

MEMORY IS A CAT

Memory is a cat. It thinks only of playing. Thinking is playing. What is playing? It is sending a ball or spool rolling across the floor, rolling, rrrrr . . . rrrro

Memory must scurry off like a mouse trying to escape, so you send the object flying into space, and crack! you jump, you trap it, it squirms and wriggles, resists the jaws of Cyclope, quick! tell him a story to distract him from his murderous intention.

Don't forget the guard posted at the entry to the stadium: he is public order's immigration and customs officer, only scenes of some utility will be allowed on the track. The who-knows-why recollections will be barred, they are good-for-nothings, interlopers.

Memory wants to look like a well-kept Armoire, how pre-sumptuous! Memory is quite the opposite, it is a jumble sale, the labyrinth to a treasure trove, a fantastic jewellery shop, a warehouse of surprises, you go from room to room, what a mar-vellous storehouse! An abundance of Everything and Nothing, even rooms full of rooms of all sizes and designs, a whole collection in which your soul may pick what best suits this or that state of mind.

So on this cloudy day of which I speak I was let into a dimly lit room in the form of a circus, already crowds jostled under the big top. Everybody wanted to be up front and centre, I fled, I was afraid to trip going down the stairs, I hung around the entryway, that is, the exit. I sat in a chair as far from the stage as possible, an ancient and heavy timidity gripped me, I am not privy to the secret, I cannot count myself among the well-adapted, I am an endangered species, a few more seconds and

most importantly, when you no longer remember, when the end is near, when you are condemned and only a few dozen metres-minutes remain before the last (metreminute), you must cling to the *idea* of saving your skin, not even the idea—there's no time—a leap, you exit chased by the guard into a downpour and to the amazement of Whoever-the-Witness you are saved by the rain: head over heels, you start to run run run the rain makes a mobile shield, run, you are about to vanish at the end of the road, no road only a wall of rain, the guard could shoot, but he'd be shooting blind, run run

And that's what I do; even if I appear to be sitting in an armchair I'm rushing from one dream to the next, I exit one dream when

I see another one coming out of the mist towards me, or from time to time when I surface between two dreams to drink a cup of coffee and suddenly hop aboard the next one, this is how I hope to escape the nightmares that prey, like an army of demented executioners, upon the so-called real world

How do they manage, people who don't have a DreamScope to conjure up their dreams, poor souls, I can't imagine life under Nightmare's bell jar. I knew freedom once. When it is pure and free you take it for granted. You come and go, get up, go to bed immortally for years, you lose track, you are neither aware nor unaware, you are distracted, you breathe in and out, enter this store, that one, there are calendars for each and every one. I need all my mental energy, I flex my imagination's muscles to estimate the state of the brains of those who have never caught a whiff of the air of liberty, lightly sugared, a touch salty, discreet, pleasant, newborns who've been caged, destined from their first to last breath to slavery's dungeons, all those whose only taste of liberty is the regret implanted in their bodies by inheritance's mystery. See this handsome black cat or monkey whose lot from birth is enclosure, this human being who will never once, in his time on earth, have scented the taste of outside air. Or who has never touched The Outside, even for a tenth of a second, such a being will live with his nose pressed against the glass, paws joined in a vain and ignorant prayer, painfully hopeful of an 'over-there, nameless, forever-and-ever unknown' there! there! what is it called, that transcendental, non-existent absence-presence that causes your breast to tremble? Might it be That, god of the cat?

I can't do without Cat, I can't think without Cat,

all cats are born free even if they have never suckled the milk of unlimited air, body in captivity, soul free

The need to go Out, after the Belly, after the Cradle, beyond the house, further than the house, beyond the territory, the Urgency to Go

this is God

the verb *Aller* [go], the French language's most irregular verb, is the god that one must madly move in order to advance several me's at once, the word that sets the French language in motion, from the room of stars to a battle, to the coal mine, the most hardworking, playful, artistic, inventive, loving, fateful word, without which time stands still, the word that gives me orders, propels me, incites me to fly, before I was a cat I was a hunter-gatherer, as a farmer I have contradictory needs

I want to go outside so I may wish to go back inside, I want to shelter inside in order to want to go outside further and further, until I feel the desire to go back inside and sit in a nut-shell and hoist the sail of a sheet of A4 paper to the mast of my Montblanc pen

In the morning I close the door of my tiny huge study, behind the door Isha cries: In! In! I open. Isha goes to the window. She cries: Out! Out!

My only thought: go to the forest in order to return to the
sea to go

right until forget the forest   until

Was that a memory? I entered the bedroom, as if the bedroom had called out to me, the bedroom on the left at the back of the house where our parents slept when they were alive and lovers, that was in another tale, do you remember?—I don't remember—the sky at the window was as blue as the sky at my window at the end of this book, the same blue, calm, fine, solid, a parcel of eternity,

a memory?

But my feeling of relief was not a memory, like drunkards my lungs

sucked up air, that intoxicating sensation of having been returned to the mysterious pleasure of living, and meanwhile out of breath, full of anxiety, for a moment before you were descending the steps of drowning, and then to find yourself—newborn! among the *Breathers*, a blow

More air!   more!—Oh, there's Mama! Such happiness! Not surprising. This is her room as it used to be, right after the world's fall, empty save for the double bed. Nothing has changed.

Climb a ladder, start to clean the closets, the paintings, even at a hundred years old, even dead, that's my mama

Or perhaps this is a dream-memory, one of the dreams that memory dreams up

Call it a résumé of my mother. Stepladders: even dead, she went on cleaning, at the risk of falling and breaking her foot

No point in asking: Mama, what on earth are you doing? She was polishing some kind of mirror, mirror filled with memories, no doubt.

Apart from the mirror hanging just below the ceiling, the bedroom hasn't changed a whit.

I don't recall when I began to sleep with my mother. That of course was after father.

We lay like spoons, my mother the spoon, me the spoonful. This is how you fill the gulf that has opened, with a teaspoon.

I don't know if it was me or my brother in the spoon's cavity. I don't know if we slept together or first one then the other. We were protecting the bed

Obviously

I don't know who was protecting whom. My mother was behind me. Together we kept the hole in the universe plugged

How long that went on for I do not know. There was no decision. There was no interruption. The spoon must have continued without our knowing it, the cork must have done its corking.

Remember? I don't remember, my mother says. Or my brother. Tell me about the little spoon?

We were trying to seal the crack in the earth's crust, I say, we were afraid Papa would slip and fall to the bottom. I was trying to wake my mother, I was using words, they were all merely noise-making words, not seeing-words, hadn't I found myself from one day to the next, a Friday, perched on the planet's torn edge, where time's fields run out? I still see the cliff, it was inflamed and bloody, so the planet's body was flesh and nerves, this vision of reality was called The Wound. The word too was bleeding. I couldn't tell my mother—

No, no I don't remember, my mother says

It was a long time ago. No, no I don't recall.

I don't have any special memory

I don't remember the exact moment my mother began to forget

Perhaps at the moment of the Wound.

Night after night I would try to open the door

We were in the big bed, in the big room in the back of the house. My mother didn't remember. She was wriggling her big toes. The rest was silence and sleep. Probably it was my parents' bed.

Maybe—my father's ghost slept with us? Was the bed not yet shaped to fit my father's long, thin, burning-with-fever body? I didn't think so.

What was his voice like? I asked. I don't recall, my mother's voice said.

The ghost of his voice in my mouth, I have my father's breath but its melody is dead, and his breath is living still

The memory of a voice? What trace of death more paltry pale fleeting, less graspable, more evasive than a dream's fitfulness

All that remains are the marginalia of the inhaled, exhaled notes of the Harmonica my mother brought to life with the energy of a midwife at the wheel of a delivery:

Breathe, push, breath, a person is coming who has never yet tasted air's strength

Do you remember Mama's Harmonica?

I try

Is this a memory? I see my mother's lips bite down on the long metal biscuit, I hear nothing. Lips like hands of a midwife.

Do I have memories? What is a memory?

My days come and go, their almost motionless river is swept with traces, am I in the river's current or on the edge? I see the shores of Lethe. The river repeats itself unchangingly, on and on, endlessly until we heave ourselves, the river and me, out.

The garden is This Garden. This garden is populated with an indefinite number of presences and visits. Seated on a bench, This Bench, I almost don't notice a furtive future thought that thinks: I was sitting on This Bench, at the corner of the house where the cat slips out of sight, where Eve my mother, seen only by my hallucinating eye, sits in her usual chair under the strawberry trees.

Memories? No memories, no reproductions of visitors in an album frozen in time but waves, glints of reflections, of instants, bits and pieces, allusions, syllables, sometimes just letters, but capitals, a swarm of winged motes, the dead are not dead, all my old cats slip by, hurried thoughts between the paths of present cats, a characteristic of this populace is incessant movement, I do not know what drives them, is it the wind, the spirits, the gods, my beating heart?

No one is dead as long as I am here to greet and traipse after them

Do you remember my Sonnet 81? Shakespeare asks, the sonnet that has kept me company from 26 May 1954 to this day 26 May 2020, we've never been apart, today is the same 26 May, between us immortality reigns, a love which does not alter

that's why we are able to remember a sonnet, inscribed in the magic stone of the book: I open Shakespeare and the young sounds of the sonnet prophetic of our mysterious future memories are inscribed on its paper lips. 'Your monument shall be my gentle verse, / Which eyes not yet created shall o'er-read.' I have never read these lines in vain, sixty-six months of May readingreading

I no longer remember when I was severed from myself. I've been living in this state of separation for so long, I move like a robot, empty, you must keep going, but not without suffering, a sludge of boredom in the bottom of me, floating on an unmarked swathe of time, time is a flat surface with no horizon, no perspective, I don't know if the shore is behind or ahead of me, I could die like this, without knowing the day, without the soothing effect of a date, lost

I no longer remember when I wrote: I've—

That's what is left to me, what is left of me. It looks like a bargain-basement syllable, but it is not nothing, it's a link that remembers a chain, it is a signature that attests I was and therefore could be

I no longer remember how long I've been submerged. At the end of a certain amount of time, eight minutes, days, pages, you rise to the surface: one step, half a second, death, life, the half-second step doesn't exist, fate severs it

I have opened the empty notebook, consulted the big yearly calendar. If I'm not mistaken today is Monday, 28 June of I don't know what year. To give myself an idea of my state of dis-junction—the muffled pain of mental starkness—I borrow a mirror from my pioneering predecessors in inner shipwrecks. Some have bequeathed accounts of out-of-body experiences to humanity. In order to pass on this quasi-posthumous message, three conditions are required: faith that the human species will survive in an unqualified future, for it is to it that you wish to speak; the courage to renounce knowledge and mastery and describe the undescribable; and three, a glass bottle with a good cork, the kind they used to make for ships at risk of foundering.

I have the mirror. It is an Edgar Allen Poe *Tale* published, as chance would have it, on a 28th of June but in 1831. I start to read it. Right away a feeling I lack the words to describe takes possession of my soul. This is it exactly, that sick feeling, that wooziness that grips me-and-everyone-else in the intolerably anguishing moments when our memories crash: nothing that happens, no detail, no object is familiar, not that you have lost them, nor that they are damaged, but because everything your eyes, ears, mind encounter has never before been perceived, you have the feeling of having been handed over, unarmed and defenceless, to madness like a gladiator with no sword to a monstrous lion. A sensation that brooks no analysis, whose translation is not to be found in the lexicons of time past, to which I fear no future, no end times will provide a key.

Like Everybody in this year of supernatural circumstances, we cling to the usual feeble clichés, coming up with a lot of end-of-the-world, apocalypse, global-catastrophes, none of which manage to stop the hole in the planet's hull.

On all sides the world is cracking. That fissures appear worldwide is both terrifying and reassuring. The whole earth is one country as in the Book of Genesis.

The planet's body is infected; from hair-thin but deep cracks millions of toxic inhumans seep. All the repressed return: omnipotent cruelties, lies, brutality, delirium

But there are roses on the balcony, my mother's voice says, and the magnolias are still in bloom.

At which point I think: luckily Mama made her exit before the calamity. And I rejoice over my afflictions. How fortunate we said goodbye before the victory of the poison death, a summer, with flowers, cats, the good old days, and without war between unalive, non-human humans, we die, first the Beloved, next my mother, next the cat Philia, and right after that cat Aletheia, I filed a complaint, I accused the Blind Invisible Cruel On-High, if we are born to lose and die, thanks but no thanks, I said

Who'd have thought the today would come when I rejoiced over these opportune exits? What anniversaries we commemorated, I choked back my tears, I stroked each beloved body, I wrapped my sleepers in murmurs and silks, I kissed the mouths of my out-of-breath beloveds, what happiness we'd had

You wouldn't believe it

When Time's doors slammed shut the cats were new born. They live much faster than we do. Within our enclosure our two temporalities ran an unequal race. For us time had almost stopped. Six months took forty years. Yet Cat Time, Time the Cat leapt at the speed of a leopard, already youth, already maturity's sheen, the cats slipped past like two svelte caravels, I saw them come and go, two fleshly Illuminations, Grace itself, the one pointing up the other, so quick so quick, that my slowed-down memory couldn't keep their quicksilver gleam.

I rose, it was still dark, as usual, with night's signature, a gold fingernail with, in the distance, the pinprick of a star, I glanced at my watch. Since yesterday, three and a half weeks had passed. I stretched out my hand for the bottle filled with the juice of my before-waking dreams. No bottle. During my incalculable absence, my bottle had been thrown into the Water of Centuries. It had left me on the shore like a pen without paper, homeless and earthless. My DreamScope, gone!—Oh! I'm lost! I am good for the bin.

I ought to have known: hadn't I stumbled over the tomb of the author of the *Journal of a Plague Year*, right where the text buried him in a parenthesis, page 232—depending on the edition you read—without ceremony without eulogies no tarrying, whereupon he picked himself up and charged off again, with none of the mood swings of a deceased who when he held the reigns would curb the Creature's high spirits.

Thus was I outshone

Disembarked. I couldn't even spot the text's sail on the horizon. *Shackleton* and *Kafka* disappear into a vaporous glitter. I was, I saw, going to forget everything before the notebook's end. I jotted down the date; today, Saturday 19 September 2020. I hadn't seen the weeks go by. Outstripped, I tell myself

'Between April and September 2020 years went by. To this airless, measureless period that seemed to me so vain and event-less, I now attach great importance, as to a distant epoch

'So different is it from all the other rests-of-my-lives that already it has that mythological soul that belongs to the most ancient tales.'

How fast Oblivion goes, as fast as Memory. Already I was no longer of this text.

Someone is writing these lines

2 August 1914–2020